WILDCAT

WILDCAT

AN APPALACHIAN ROMANCE

JEFFREY DUNN

IZZARD INK
PUBLISHING®

IZZARD INK PUBLISHING
www.izzardink.com

Library of Congress Cataloging-in-Publication Data

Names: Dunn, Jeffrey, 1956- author.
Title: Wildcat : an Appalachian romance / a novel by Jeffrey Dunn.
Description: First edition. | Salt Lake City : Izzard Ink Publishing, 2024.
Identifiers: LCCN 2023052600 (print) | LCCN 2023052601 (ebook) | ISBN
9781642280982 (hardback) | ISBN 9781642280975 (paperback) | ISBN
9781642280999 (ebook other) | ISBN 9781642282023 (ebook)
Subjects: LCSH: Appalachian Region–Fiction. | LCGFT: Fictional
autobiographies. | Novels.
Classification: LCC PS3604.D5586 W55 2024 (print) | LCC PS3604.D5586
(ebook) | DDC 813/.6–dc23/eng/20231222
LC record available at https://lccn.loc.gov/2023052600
LC ebook record available at https://lccn.loc.gov/2023052601

Designed by Daniel Lagin
Cover Design by Andrea Ho

First Edition
Contact the author at inchitensee@gmail.com
Paperback ISBN: 978-1-64228-097-5
Hardback ISBN: 978-1-64228-098-2
Audiobook ISBN: 978-1-64228-099-9
eBook ISBN: 978-1-64228-202-3

for my friends

in the Rust Belt

of the Appalachians

CONTENTS

WILDCAT

THE DAM

CAROLYN

LOST SURREAL INTERLUDE

WILDCAT

TAKING STOCK

I 've come back to Wildcat. I say "back" because I've lived here before, the first time for only a year. It was my senior year of high school. My father managed small manufacturing firms, and as this was the time of America's great industrial failure, we moved quite a bit, hopping from one ill-fated factory town to another. I'm not proud to say my father closed a lot of mills and sent a lot of men home. And now I've retired to Wildcat.

Wildcat is not a place people retire to. Most old people in the Rust Belt of Appalachia were born here and then never left. Interlopers are rare, even ones like me who lived here for a short time. I feel like a bloomed-out iris in a patch of Wildcat mayapples. And despite all that, I'm back.

Despite the catastrophic changes that rocked Wildcat my senior year.

Despite the mine explosion.

Despite the funeral for the miners who were killed, one of them my friend Dominic's brother.

Despite the closing of the mill (and, yes, my father had a hand in that).

Despite the fire at the mill and then the unthinkable thing that happened after the fire was put out.

Despite the way I left, ending the relationship with my first love Carolyn, the girl with whom I explored the hill and the river and the creek, not to mention our art, our feelings and our bodies, the girl who kept me honest and the girl I left behind.

Yes, despite all that I've returned because my old friend Dominic said I should come back. He told me about Wildcat's magical changes, ones so different from the disastrous ones of the past. He said I needed to see for myself, like how he had started a mushroom farm in the mine where his brother was killed.

Like how the mill that my father closed was now a workshop for artisans, a place where paper was being made from mushrooms, furniture and household utensils from sassafras, and honey and candles from beehives.

Like how the once failed Hotel Wildcat was now a thriving collective living and dining space. Dominic said that there was a room for me in Hotel Wildcat, and I have to say, the picture he painted of Wildcat was exactly the sort of place where a writer, dreamer, loner like me could be happy.

Like how Carolyn had recently returned to Wildcat after all these years. Dominic also said that I had unfinished business with Carolyn. To be honest, I wasn't sure what he meant. I mean, Carolyn and I felt finished fifty years ago, but since this was Dominic, it was something I couldn't ignore.

INTRODUCTIONS

Looking back over what I've written, I see an introduction. Maybe it's an introduction to unfinished business, an account of what's in store for Carolyn and me. It could be the story of two people reconciling after many years. Or possibly Faulkner was right all along, that digging for treasure only leads to an empty hole.

But it also might be an introduction to one Appalachian town's renewal. Dominic not only told me about Carolyn but also about the changes that have come to Wildcat, and if I'm to write an account of those changes, the place to start is with Hotel Wildcat, my new home.

Hotel Wildcat is two stories tall with a pitched attic roof. It has hemlock clapboards and chestnut bones. There is a lobby door cut on the diagonal and a tavern door facing In Street. A long time ago, someone looked at the coal seam that ran along the hill and dug the mine, constructed the mill to smelt iron, put in the railroad, and built the dam. Soon to follow were houses, the school, and the church, and soon after that, the hotel, the place for those with little means and simple ways to gather, get drunk, and be on display. Someone named it Hotel Wildcat.

My second-floor room in Hotel Wildcat has three windows. Two front windows bring in the morning light from the river. A third side window frames Wildcat. It's the picture I like best.

If I go to the front windows, I can see the river. Today, the river's water is gray, and the clouds are threatening like an old tombstone with the word "INFANT" carved on its weathered face.

I sleep on a worn chaise longue. It was new once, and then someone didn't want it anymore, it went out with the trash, so a few days back I carried it home and had the bed removed. I've never cared much for things, especially new things. Some have said I was born against the grain of the American Dream. I recall my mother using words to that effect. My father never said such things. I don't think he felt the need.

I sit on a chair covered with faux leather made from mushrooms and write on a table topped with sassafras. Both are constructed from unique materials, and they were made here in Wildcat. It's interesting how Wildcat is using local materials and sustainable methods to turn "making do" into "making a living."

I light my room with beeswax candles made by Floreandra the beekeeper. When I sit in their light, I hear a gentle buzzing, a symphony of bees. I'm not interested in the buzz of coal fires. That is something I prefer not to hear. Around here, the sound of coal fires sounds like families at funerals and children with empty bellies.

If I leave my room, I can go across In Street and onto Wildcat Beach. There are some big chunks of concrete on top of many small rocks. I like to stop at the river and watch the ripples lap against the pebbles, continually pulling them downstream like the wind in my dreams.

Since I've been back, I've wondered where the sand on Wildcat Beach has gone. I've wondered if it has something to do with the chunks of concrete scattered here and downstream, a result of the time someone blew a hole in the dam.

Change is such an iffy affair. Sometimes it gets out of hand, and we go to places we regret. There's no guarantee.

ROCCO

When I finished writing a possible introduction, I went for a walk around Wildcat, and now that I'm back, I'm writing about some of Wildcat's past and present changes. You might think that writing about my walk, a stroll that will take place over a single day, is just a literary device. You might suspect that I didn't go for a walk at all. When I think about it, you and I need an element of trust, some faith that I actually took a walk. And surely there's an element of suspense, too, the question of whether I might have run into Carolyn. After all, Dominic did say she was back in town.

My walk began when I left Hotel Wildcat and crossed Out Street. The sun was burning through the morning gray, and a few colors said hello: the green of a shipping container, the peach on a clapboard house, the red, white, and blue hanging from a faded yellow aluminum awning.

After crossing Out Street, I went into the mill. I thought I'd say hi to Rocco. He's a few years older than me and at one time worked as an iron furnace operator. When the mill closed, he drank a bit, but then he stopped drinking (he said it wasn't helping him at all), and then he decided to make paper instead.

Rocco's workshop is in the front of the mill. He has a special process for grinding shelf fungus and turning it into paper. I particularly like the way his paper takes the ink brewed by Arabelle the ink maker. I use a turkey quill when I write. It's an interesting process, and a subject I plan to return to later.

"Hey," Rocco said. He looked up from his paper frames and over his horn-rimmed glasses. "Need something to scratch?"

"No," I said.

"What, then? Got an itch?"

"Can't say that I do," I said again.

"No itch, no scratch, then what?"

"Just thought I'd roll through."

"Don't know about you, but I feel a wind running up the river," Rocco said, still looking over his glasses. I like talking to Rocco. He's full of metaphors and keeps me on my toes.

"Up the river, you say, not down?" I asked.

"Yep."

"Do tell," I said.

"A wind that runs like a girl."

"Oh, really? Go on."

"That's all I got," Rocco said. He just kept looking over his glasses. He is a damn good poker player. "You'll need to go up the river and drop in a line if you want to catch more than swirls."

THE SASSAFRAS WORKS

After chatting with Rocco, I walked through the mill, a place that once smelted iron but now is home to small businesses. I thought I'd say hi to Floreandra and chat with her, maybe find out what was afoot with Carolyn, but first I had to pass by the sassafras works.

As I made my way, I could hear sawing and planing going on. Sunlight came through the wall facing the river and the other wall facing the hill. These walls once had been covered in galvanized metal sheeting, siding that had fallen away long ago. Only the steel posts and beams, along with the roof, remained.

A yellow-orange sun cut through the wood dust suspended over the workspace. Above the rafters was dark, but below was a luminous layer of smoky amber.

I stopped for a moment and watched Dougie and Terence. Dougie was working the saw, and Terence was feeding him sassafras. They were cutting raw sassafras logs into lengths.

Sassafras is a member of the laurel family and gives off a sweet, spicy smell, especially when fresh. Those who work in this shop shape sassafras into beds and chests and tables and chairs and bowls and plates and spoons and forks— things which are now becoming part of Wildcat.

I nodded to Dougie and Terence, and they nodded back. They both wore trucker caps and were born after I left Wildcat.

Then, I walked over to Chéri. I picked up a length of sassafras off a pile, and when Chéri turned to grab another, she saw me and gave me that mock frown, the one I've come to expect, and I handed her the length.

When Chéri finished planing the sassafras, she turned off the machine. "Hey, stranger," she said. Her greeting was really a joke because my passing through was becoming routine.

"Just stopped by for the usual, a good dose of aromatherapy."

"Well, boss, smell away."

That was another joke because no one is Chéri's boss, least ways me, the guy who lives above the lobby of Hotel Wildcat. "I was just wondering," I began. "How long have you been here, at the sassafras works, I mean?"

"Ever since we started up."

"I wasn't here, then."

"No, you left a long time ago."

"True, true, but I was here for all the trouble. Most of it, at least."

"Yeah, I was really little when all that started. Just a seedling for sure. I remember seeing a broken-down school bus and the people from the bus setting up a big tent below the hill. They were behind the mill on that same patch of ground where Floreandra has her hives and Anthony has his garden. I remember the music they played at night when I went to sleep."

"What sort of music?"

"Couldn't say. That kind of music was new to me. A *babcia* told me it was gypsy music, violins and an accordion. Sometimes I'd hear a guy singing, and sometimes it was a girl. I always liked when they sang together. I liked those songs best."

"I lived up on the hill then."

"Yeah, you're older than me. You left right after the trouble."

"That's true," I said.

"Do you remember their music?" she asked.

"Yeah, I heard them play once."

"Well, sometimes at night I have trouble sleeping, so I remember one of their songs, one with the guy and girl singing together, and before I know it, I'm fast asleep, just like when I was a kid."

EVERYTHING STOPPED

Just then, right when Chéri finished telling me about her difficulties sleeping, everything stopped. The grind from the planer stopped. The whirring that came from the power saw, the one that was cutting sassafras, stopped. The sound of children playing in the schoolyard stopped.

LUNCH

The chat I wanted to have with Floreandra, the one where I might go upstream and drop in a line, would have to wait. It was time for one of Wildcat's many changes, the time for lunch when many Wildcat people leave their places of work, go home, and share a meal with others.

Some people don't go home for lunch. Many of the children at the school eat lunch with their teachers. They could walk home, and some do, those who have someone alone at home, but children who have a home filled with this infant and that grandma, and don't forget Mom and Dad, these children don't go home. They stay and keep their teachers company.

Other people go to the church for lunch. These folks live where no one comes home. For them, everything stops for lunch, and they leave their homes. Some come from

Wildcat, and others walk down from the hill. The church is where they have lunch together. It's a new Wildcat tradition.

I take my meals at Hotel Wildcat, as does everyone else who lives here. When the moment comes, we make our way to the hotel from wherever we are. We enter the tavern and sit at the sassafras tables on the mushroom leather-covered chairs.

Donald and Alexander do the cooking. They also manage Hotel Wildcat. No one owns Hotel Wildcat, but Donald and Alexander came back to Wildcat to manage this place and cook for those like me who have rooms here.

When I entered the tavern, I smelled fresh baked bread. A large bowl of mushroom soup, *zupa grzybowa* the babcias call it, steamed on each table. Many different sorts of pickles—sweet, hot, dill, candied cinnamon, and Hungarian—were on display. Donald and Alexander are high priests of the pickle, and as such, we who eat here are daily blessed.

Each table also had a pitcher of ice-cold milk and a plate of sweet, golden butter. Our milk and butter come from the dairy, a farm which extends along the river in the floodplain that was created after someone blew a hole in the dam. The dairy is populated by Jersey cows. Their butter is very rich.

Every morning the dairy's keepers, Mary Kay and John, milk the cows and then let them out to pasture. The cows' bells chime for many miles up and down the river and onto the hill.

Every evening the cows return to be milked. Their bells start up again, and all heaven rings out across Wildcat.

DOMINIC'S MUSHROOMS

L unch for me started when I sat down and passed the bread to Arabelle. She took a slice and then scooped some butter and spread it on the slice.

I watched as Leonard ladled soup into a sassafras bowl. We went to school together, and now he lives down the hall from me. His grandfather once had a ferry service rowing people across the river before the dam was built, and his father worked as the school's custodian. One day, his father had a heart attack and died with a toilet plunger in his hand. Some say he died in the line of duty. Later, Leonard took his father's place as the school's custodian, and he is beloved around here because everyone has a childhood memory of Leonard magically appearing and cleaning up their innocent vomits and bloody noses. In a way, Leonard also has been the school nurse for the last forty years because the school can't afford a nurse of its own.

Once Leonard had filled his bowl, Dominic came in and sat down next to me. He reopened the mine a few years back. For many years before that, the mine was closed because of an accident. There was an explosion, part of the mine collapsed, and a few miners were killed. At the time, we didn't know that many more terrible things were to follow.

Luigi Vitali, Valentin Milasky, and Abernathy Collie were the three men who were killed. Luigi was Dominic's older brother, and Dominic was not only Carolyn's and my good friend, but Arabelle's, too. Dominic told me the cause after it happened. He said that Luigi and Valentin were using a carbide lamp to light their way, and the lamp's flame accidentally ignited a blasting cartridge.

He also told me that Abernathy Collie wasn't with Luigi and Valentin but in a different part of the mine. After the explosion, Abernathy was able to get to the adit, which is the main passage out of the mine, but it didn't help Abernathy any, because there was too much gas.

A few years before I came back, I was surprised when Dominic wrote to me about reopening the mine. He said he wanted to wall off the areas affected by the collapse and start to grow mushrooms in the undamaged galleries. I was surprised because I thought he would have stayed away, what with his brother being killed there. In his letter, he said he wasn't so sure about the idea either, but he figured that something good should come from his brother's death. He said it was his way of moving on.

Since my return, I've learned that Dominic's mushrooms are a hit in Wildcat. He also grows mycelium in leftovers from the sassafras works. He has found a way to mold mycelium and sassafras into shapes, and then he sends these shapes back to the sassafras works, the place where one thing naturally becomes another in ways that nurture Wildcat every day.

"Hey, Dominic, how are you and the mushrooms getting along?" I asked. "I hear they're a pretty unruly bunch."

"No, we're fine," Dominic said. "I got something else on my mind." He's my oldest friend, so I was interested in what he had to say.

"What's that?" Arabelle asked. She handed Dominic the bread, and Leonard ladled another bowl of soup.

"It's The Shadows. I saw a new one today."

"The Shadows?" I asked.

"Yeah, the mine has more than its share, what with the accident and all."

"You say you saw a new one?" I followed up.

"Yeah, this one was different."

"Different how?" Arabelle asked. She spread more butter on her bread, although the slice she held was already buttered.

"This one glowed. It was like it was wearing a robe of light. And it was smaller, too."

"Sounds pretty mysterious. I've never seen one that was wearing a robe, certainly not one made of light," Leonard said, passing a bowl of soup to Dominic, who almost spilled the soup, but he didn't. Dominic leveled the bowl just in time.

"Me neither," Dominic said, and then he paused. He seemed to be waiting for something to come to mind, but instead of saying something else, he started to eat his soup. I guess he had nothing else to say.

ARABELLE

When lunch was over, Arabelle and I took a walk. I like Arabelle. She is Carolyn's oldest friend and was born in Wildcat. Her parents ran the store, and the children always stopped there to buy candy. It was a daily occurrence. The children would leave the school to get the mail and stop for candy on the way back. It was always a different class, and the principal gave the children coins to trade for sweets. The children would follow their teacher like ducklings to the post office, *quack*, and to the store, *quack, quack*, and back to the school, *quack, quack, quack*.

But after I left, the store burned. The post office closed and was left to the termites. And now Arabelle lives across the hall from me in Hotel Wildcat and brews ink from mushrooms.

Our walk took us out from Hotel Wildcat toward the hill. We didn't go toward Wildcat or the dairy, and the river was at our backs. We walked toward the mine, but before we got there, we turned, walked a short way, turned back again, and climbed a draw only used by 'possums and deer. Then, we found ourselves above the mine looking down upon all that lay along the river.

"What brought you back?" Arabelle asked.

"Dominic."

"Oh, come on. It's been a long time, but I don't remember you as someone who does something just because somebody says so. Sure, I love Dominic dearly, but I don't do stuff just because he says so."

"Okay, Arabelle, you got me there. I'm not lying, though. I did take Dominic up on his invitation. I guess what you really want to know is *why*."

"You said it. I didn't." Her smile helped me continue.

"The story is that, before I retired, I thought about where, and when I was done thinking, I decided on Wildcat."

"That's the stupidest thing I've ever heard. You lived here for only a year. It was the worst year Wildcat ever had, and it was a *very* long time ago. I live here because this is home, and if I know one thing about you, Wildcat's not your home."

"It is now."

"Oh, really?" And there it was, sarcasm.

"I think it has a lot to do with my dad never having a job for more than three years, and then when he changed jobs, we'd move. We lived in a lot of houses, but we were never anywhere long enough for it to feel like home. Then after Wildcat, I went to state college, and after college, I bounced around from one teaching job to another and from one wife to another, but I'm not complaining. I'm really not. I've always been low maintenance. I'm fine with just a roof, heat, and some food. In the evening, all I need is a walk and some time to read and write. Even you've got to admit that I've got all that right here."

"I'm not buying it. No, you're not lying, but I'm still not buying it."

"You want more?"

"Come on, spill it. Dominic and I are still good friends, you know."

"Okay, Dominic did tell me that Wildcat is a very different place now. And he was right. I'm very comfortable here, no complications. I really like my single room in Hotel Wildcat. When I'm in my room, I feel like I'm in a Buddhist monastery. I've read all the hits like *A Buddhist Bible*, *The Life of Milarepa*, and *The Lotus Sutra*. I especially like *The Diamond Sutra*, very to the point."

"Now you're quoting book titles? You could be a Buddhist lots of places. What else did Dominic tell you?"

"That Carolyn's back."

"Ooooh, now you're talking."

"Is that what you wanted to know? Is my mystery solved?"

"Oh, I don't know that it was ever a mystery, at least not for me and Dominic."

"Maybe not, but now it's your turn," I said changing the subject. "Tell me exactly how you turn water into wine."

"It's not how, it's what."

"What kind of mushrooms, you mean?"

"That's where it starts."

"Is Dominic any help?" I was curious. She did say that she and Dominic were still friends after all these years.

"He doesn't grow shaggy manes."

"Shaggy manes?"

"Yeah, shaggy manes. They deliquesce."

"Deli, what?"

"Deliquesce. They turn to black mush. Then, they dissolve."

"Wow. Who knew?"

"Me." She hadn't lost her sparkle.

"True, true, but what about the how?"

"It takes about two weeks, but they stink a bit. For that, I add a bit of my homemade thyme oil."

"Then you got wine?"

"Yep, *we* got wine. That is, if you want to help."

"Sure." It all seemed very enchanting.

"Okay, let's do a little mushroom hunting."

"How's that?"

"We'll start by following this rise, then hook up with Out Street and follow it down to Wildcat. Shaggy manes like well-traveled trails and roadsides."

"But how will I know when I see one?"

"It's all in the name, silly. All in the name."

SHAGGY MANES

Arabelle and I walked along. We stopped and admired a family of small, creamy-fringed umbrellas pushed up from the soil. I handed her my Barlow knife, and she exposed the blade.

MY WRITING

After we returned to Hotel Wildcat, Arabelle and I delivered the shaggy manes to her room. I watched while she carefully laid them out on her sassafras-topped table.

I had enjoyed our afternoon together—"Thanks, Arabelle"—and then went back to my room.

When I closed the door, I felt disordered, so I collected my papers and put my turkey feathers back in a box made by Dougie at the sassafras works. Since I've returned to Wildcat, I've been writing with a turkey quill dipped in Arabelle's mushroom ink. I haven't always written this way. For a long time, I wrote like most people. I used a computer keyboard, but after I moved into Hotel Wildcat, I thought I'd try writing with something else.

I think this change goes back to the time one teacher gave me a big, round, wooden pencil and showed me how to print. Then, another teacher took away my pencil and said, "Use this pen. And stop printing. You need to learn cursive. This is cursive. *Look*. Now follow along and write the way I do. Ready, ready, ready, *write*."

I didn't care much for cursive. It hurt my hand. I tried,

but some of my letters were connected and some of them weren't, and over time, I became the Doctor Frankenstein of cursive.

Fortunately, I learned to type and, of course, I was thrilled when computers and word processing came along, but when I came back to Wildcat, I thought I'd start collecting turkey feathers, the ones I found scattered about the hill. I thought that it might be a good writing implement, and as I'd heard that people once had written with feathers, well, there it was.

The last few days, Rocco has taught me that changing feathers into writing implements is a bit of an art. The process starts with me getting a good fire going. I like to use hickory, maybe sassafras in a pinch. Some swear by apple wood, but any old hardwood will do.

Then, I cure the quill in the hot ashes, only the ashes, not the coals, and certainly not the flame. I don't want to burn or scorch the quill, just soften it.

Once I've got the quill the way I like it, I take out my Barlow knife, open the blade, and use its cheek to shape the quill. Next, I employ the edge to give the quill a trim, and when the quill is ready for use, I don't hold it near the end. Instead, I hold it farther up the shaft, the way Monet held his brush.

This is to say, my writing isn't writing at all; what I'm doing now is painting. The thing is, painting doesn't hurt my hand.

A Good Question

Once I'd put my room back in order, I felt better. When I feel out of kilter, I try to remember that my thoughts and feelings are affected by simple conditions like yesterday's shirt lying on the floor, an abandoned building, or a thing someone said.

Then, I remembered Chéri asking me, "Do you remember their music?" so I recalled the gypsy songs Chéri was referring to and began to remember the time after the mill closed. My parents had left Wildcat for my father's new job, and I was leaving soon for college. I had just sat down to dinner. I had prepared sloppy joes, and there was a basket of potato chips, and the condiments were arranged in the middle of the table in barnyard fashion. Right when I scooped up some sloppy joe mix to put on a bun, I heard something rhythmic, and then I heard an accordion, and soon a violin started up.

I put the spoon back into the bowl and got up and went out on the porch to see who was making music.

A group of people had gathered in our front yard. Three musicians stood together, and as they played, others danced around them. When the song ended, two dancers joined the musicians. These two smiled at me, and one of them, a man, began to sing, and then the other one, a woman, began to sing, too, and before I knew it, the musicians joined in. The performers were like the headwaters of a river, many springs of sound joining into a river of song.

When the song ended, the man stopped singing and said, *"Sa e manušikane strukture bijandžona tromane thaj jekhutne ko digniteti thaj capipa."*

I didn't understand the man's words, but I smiled. I didn't know what else to do.

Then the woman said, "All human beings are born free and equal in dignity and rights."

I cocked my head like a puppy who was waiting to see what comes next.

"Hello," the man said.

"Hi," I said.

"Hello," the woman said.

"Hi," I said.

"We here to help," the man said.

"Help?" I asked.

"Help," the woman said.

"We help your father to start again the mill," the man said.

"Oh," I said.

"He is the boss, no?" the man asked.

"Not exactly," I said.

"Not exactly?" the man asked again, but this time his question wasn't rhetorical. This time it was incredulous.

"Well, he wasn't the owner, just the manager. His job was to do whatever the owner said. He and my mother are gone."

"Gone, how is it possible?" the man asked.

"They've gone to work someplace else."

"Gone? But you live on the hill," the woman said.

"Yes, but my parents are gone, and I'm leaving in a few days for college. We don't live here anymore."

"We not help to start the mill?" the man asked.

"No."

"No?" the woman asked.

"No," I said.

"And why is it not possible?" the man asked.

"That's a good question. Like I said, my dad doesn't own the mill."

"Who owns?" the woman asked.

"I don't know. All I know is that I'm leaving on Sunday, and I won't be back."

"But the mill, it stop. No one works. Better if we start the mill, no?" the man asked.

"I suppose."

"When things are bad, we play music and dance, and we are better."

"I see what you're saying. I really do, but I'm leaving here on Sunday."

"Oh."

Then, the man and the woman turned to the others, and they all began to wind down off the hill and return to their encampment.

By Sunday evening both our house on the hill and the encampment behind the mill were empty.

KNOCK

After I finished remembering the musicians' visit, there was a knock at my door. I wondered who it might be. I wasn't accustomed to receiving visitors. I saw people at lunch, or they saw me when I walked about. There really wasn't any reason for someone to come knocking.

Knock, knock, knock. I guessed whoever it was really wanted to see me. Maybe this person thought I was taking a nap, and if one *knock* wouldn't work, then, *knock, knock, knock* might do the trick.

I found the entire situation curious, what with me sitting and remembering in my room above the lobby of Hotel Wildcat, and now someone was outside my door, knocking. It's not that I didn't want anyone to come and see me, or even that I had something against opening the door, but possibly the person would go away, *step, step, step,* and then something more important would come up, and the incident would be lost as if no one had knocked at all.

But the more I thought about it, the less it mattered, so I got up and opened the door. It was Floreandra.

FLOREANDRA

Floreandra keeps bees and makes candles. Her workshop is at the back of the mill, and her hives are just beyond that. She has a button nose, and her laughter calls to her bees and then sends them on their way.

She was born after the terrible changes that came to Wildcat. She lives upstairs in her family home, and her mother lives downstairs. Her father once worked in the mill, but then he was laid off. He tried this and failed, and then he tried that and failed, and then he tried to leave Wildcat. No one knows what became of him. Maybe he's still about in the form of The Shadow outside the mill waiting to go home for lunch. Maybe he's still waiting for a fried jumbo sandwich with a large Hungarian pickle.

On this particular day, she was wearing green denim overalls and a violet Breton cap. Her hair was long and hung in a single French braid.

"What gives, old man? I light your world," Floreandra said, "and paint your sweet tooth, and you can't walk an extra fifty feet to say hi?"

"Wow, a bit harsh, don't you think?" I asked back.

"Is it? Or is it just a hard, cold fact?"

"Both."

"Both, hmm . . ." and she paused to consider how best to hold two truths in her single, tiny hand ". . . all I got to say is that the truth will set you free."

"Not if I'm guilty."

"Hmm . . . well, give a man a lie, put out his light; teach a man to lie, put out the sun."

"Shit, Floreandra!"

"Nah, just messin' with you, old man."

"Really?"

"Yes and no."

"What's the yes?"

"The yes is you didn't stop by. The no is I'll let it slide."

"You're a generous soul."

"It's been said."

"Hey, now that you're here," I said changing the subject, "Dominic tells me Carolyn's back in town."

"What's this thing with you and Carolyn?" She looked curious or maybe annoyed, possibly both.

"Well, it's kind of a long story."

"I'll bet it is. You up for honey duty?"

"Sure."

"Good, let's go. You can whistle me your sad tale while we work."

MY SAD TALE

Instead of going through the mill, I followed Floreandra around the mill to the back, and when we got to her hives, she said, "Hail soup pot full of comb, your bees are with you. Blessèd is the sweet of your honey. Blessèd is the wax from your hives, Gobnait. Holy Pollen, Purveyor of Swarms, pray for us keepers, now and at the hour of extraction."

"Amen," I added. It only seemed appropriate.

"Okay, so whistle me the sad tale of you and Lady Carolyn," Floreandra smiled and then she lit her smoker, the device she uses to calm her bees. "You know, I've never met her. She left before I was born, or so I've been told."

"Oh, I didn't realize that."

"Well, now you do," and she sent a puff of smoke into one of her hives.

"My sad story starts before you were born, the time when I wandered lonely as a cloud."

"Oh, that's rich," and she heated a large carving knife.

"Isn't it? That floated high over the river and the hill."

"Got it" and she removed the hive's cover, pulled out a frame, and began to cut away the wax cap protecting the honey below.

"When all at once, I saw a girl who gave me thrills, along the river next to Wildcat, enchanting and tempting to look at."

"Now I'm getting bored. More story, less poetry," and she cut chunks of honeycomb from the frame.

"Sure, sure, so I was afraid to ask her out because I lived on the hill, and she lived in Wildcat. Back then, I knew my way around girls on the hill, but Wildcat girls, well, that was completely different. I was afraid they'd say *no*. I didn't want to get laughed at, but there was something interesting about them, too. I didn't really understand Wildcat girls, and I suppose that made them interesting. Obviously, I needed to get over myself. Nothing ventured, nothing gained, right?"

"True, true, so you asked her out," and she crushed the honeycomb with a potato masher.

"Well, not at first. You see, it all began when I walked her home after school one day and asked about her books. Back then, she always had a copy of *The Aquarian Gospel* and another book that always changed. One time she had *Damien*. Another time she had *Johnny Got His Gun*. Then, there was *Steppenwolf,* and later she had *Siddhartha*. I guess she had a thing for Herman Hesse."

"So, you liked her books. What else? I'm not much of a reader, so what else?"

"I think I've always been a sucker for a woman with bangs, but Carolyn never had bangs. When it came to her, it didn't matter because I really liked her ways."

"Such as?"

"I liked her long cinnamon hair and the way she parted it down the middle. I liked her color-patterned socks. I liked the way her large wire-rimmed glasses magnified her sky-blue eyes. I liked the pictures she drew, and she liked my stories. I think we saw each other as a way out. And the rest is history."

"Not so fast, old man. The way I hear it, the rest was history until it wasn't" and she poured the honeycomb mash into a strainer.

"Oh, you want me to go there, huh?"

"There and then some. You don't get off that easy."

"Seems I'm singing for my supper."

"If by supper, you mean a jar of honey."

"Deal. The thing is, Carolyn and I were together when all the terrible changes came to Wildcat. We went to school together and made love on the hill and along the river, all of it while the mine exploded, the mill closed, and someone blew a hole in the dam."

"I heard Carolyn's brother lit the fuse," and she put the remaining comb back into the soup pot and turned up the heat.

"That's true."

"Then . . ." and she skimmed off the wax that had floated to the top.

"Then, Carolyn got pregnant."

"All that love-making, old man."

"And then the abortion."

NOW

"Oh," and Floreandra poured some honey into a jar, "sorry, I didn't know."

"Well, now you do."

"Now I do."

"But all that's old news, and I want some *real* news," I said changing the subject again, "like I hear you might know something about Carolyn coming back to Wildcat."

"My mom says Carolyn moved back into her old house. I heard her mom died a few years back, and now she's got the place to herself."

"That's all?"

"That's all," and she handed me the jar, one that once

contained black raspberry jam, and then someone emptied it, the last of the jam spread on buttered toast, and now the jar was filled with honey, the sweet that came from Floreandra's bees.

WALK

I thanked Floreandra for the honey. I'd learned all she had to tell me about Carolyn. I looked out from the mill and over Floreandra's hives. Then, I looked up the river and was suddenly sad, so I thought I'd take my jar of honey and sadness down along the river.

I didn't go the way I came, around the mill on the side facing the hill. Instead, I went around on the side facing the river. When I got to the front of the mill, the circle was complete.

I continued along the river past Hotel Wildcat. I could smell good things on the breeze. Donald and Alexander were in the kitchen making dinner, and I tried to guess what that might be. I smelled yeasty bread, maybe dinner rolls. There was a garlicky smell, maybe eggs Florentine. The eggs would be tossed with chanterelles and ramps, what we call our wild onions, very unique, and the entire mixture would be sprinkled with cheese from the dairy. And maybe there would be a dandelion salad with some watercress and a bit of wood sorrel. No, I couldn't smell the salad, but I could hope. It's a favorite of mine. It has a fresh taste and is from the place I've returned to.

The sun was starting down, and the angle of light reflected off the river and burned my eyes. I turned away from the river and walked toward the hill. The dairy passed on my right, and the forest came over top like an unexpected sleep.

I walked among serviceberries and chokecherries and came upon a stand of birch followed by red maples with a few hickories. There was an oak here and another over there, but there were mostly maples with a few hickories. And the sassafras were everywhere.

THIS WAY

I knew that if I went under these trees, through this black raspberry thicket, and along this shaley cliff, I would come to the mine.

Just outside the entrance, I saw The Shadows.

THE SHADOWS

Not everyone can see The Shadows, but of those who can, a few prefer not to. As it turns out, I'm not one of those.

The Shadows started for me when my parents moved to the hill. Back then, I liked to explore. I walked up and down and across the hill. Sometimes I stopped at a particular spot and stood or sat, or I lay down for ten minutes or possibly twenty, and maybe even an hour would pass. Sometimes I came back and stopped again, and other times I stopped only once. It's not something I thought a lot about, just something I liked to do.

I saw my first one near the mine entrance. This was before the mine accident that killed Dominic's brother, but as this was a mine, earlier accidents had occurred, and other men had been killed. I was walking under some trees and along another shaley cliff when there it was: The Shadow. At first, I didn't know what it was, maybe a slag pile from the mine, or possibly a drunk had left Hotel Wildcat and come here to pass out.

As I came closer, I thought, no, it wasn't a slag pile. More likely, it was a passed out drunk, but I still wasn't sure. The color wasn't quite right, and there was a certain transparency, the way someone standing behind a sheer curtain appears to someone looking from the street.

Then, I remembered hearing stories, ones about The Shadows told by kids who lived in Wildcat. At the time, I didn't take their stories seriously. Oh, their stories were interesting in that around-the-campfire sort of way, but The Shadows? Come on!

But here it was, my first one, and I thought about reevaluating the stories that Wildcat kids told. Could it be that scientists and politicians didn't know everything, and certainly not some kid like me on the hill, one who took long, aimless walks and stood for hours thinking about heaven knows what.

And as I stood there reevaluating, sounds sprouted in my head. I wasn't sure what to make of them. I thought it might be a voice, so I tried to understand the words. I thought it was like a whisper, but then not really. Or maybe it was like something on the wind, but it was only in my head. I had no way of knowing. Whatever it was sounded like somebody's name, but I couldn't make out what it was.

All this happened to me a long time ago, the time when The Shadow first appeared to me outside the mine, but now I was well acquainted with The Shadows, especially The Shadow of Luigi Vitali, Dominic's brother, and just behind him, The Shadow of Valentin Milasky. I felt an everlasting patience as I always did when I stopped by The Shadows. There was nothing creepy about them, and if I put my hand in, I felt a pleasant chill.

I began to chant, "Luigi Luigi, Luigi Vitali. Valentin Valentin, Valentin Milasky. Luigi Luigi, Luigi Vitali. Valentin Valentin, Valentin Milasky. Luigi Luigi, Luigi Vitali. Valentin Valentin, Valentin Milasky," and then I stopped. When I turned toward the mine entrance, Dominic was there, waiting.

THE ONE WHO STAYED

"Goofing with The Shadows?" Dominic asked.
"You might say that," I said.
"Hmm."

"Hmm yourself."

"They got much to say?" Dominic asked.

"Can't say they do," I said.

"Didn't think so. Silent types, huh?"

"Pretty much."

"Luigi, right?" I asked. I thought it important to acknowledge that Luigi had been Dominic's brother.

"Yeah."

"And Valentin. Remind me, did you know him before the mine exploded?"

"Valentin was older," Dominic said. "I saw him around, but I didn't know him. Him and Luigi got blown against a wall in the mine. There was nothing to rescue. They dumped their bodies right outside."

"Sad."

"You got that right."

"And Abernathy Collie?" I asked.

"Abernathy," Dominic nodded down toward The Shadow of Abernathy. "The explosion didn't get him. White damp did."

"White damp?"

"Mine gas, mostly carbon monoxide," Dominic explained.

"Sad."

"Even sadder was he left six kids behind. They all lived in Wildcat, and then they didn't."

"He's the only one who stayed, huh?"

"You could say that."

WHAT I DIDN'T WANT

After saying goodbye to Dominic, I passed by The Shadow of Abernathy Collie and only stopped long enough to chant, "Abernathy Abernathy, Abernathy Collie. Abernathy Abernathy, Abernathy Collie. Abernathy Abernathy, Abernathy Collie."

Then I looked down at the jar of honey in my hand, the honey that Floreandra's bees had worked so hard to make, and I knew I'd better head back for dinner. I knew Donald and Alexander would soon bring out bowls of good things to eat, and I didn't want them to worry. They might wonder if I was mad at someone, possibly Donald or maybe even Alexander. I didn't want that at all.

DINNER

Dinner at Hotel Wildcat was good in the Wildcat way: Wildcat dishes prepared by Donald and Alexander from Wildcat ingredients for Wildcat people.

The good things I smelled earlier were already piled in sassafras bowls on sassafras-topped tables. There were yeasty dinner rolls and eggs Florentine with chanterelles and ramps in compound butter and sprinkled with cheese from the dairy. And there was a dandelion salad with watercress and wood sorrel, this time topped with black locust and wild rose petals.

All the residents of Hotel Wildcat were already there. Arabelle smiled up from the dinner roll she was buttering. Leonard raised a chanterelle on his sassafras fork in greeting. Dominic was busily serving himself some dandelion salad. Somehow, he had gotten down the hill before me. I don't know how he did it, but he did.

"What brought you back this time?" That Arabelle!

"Good food," I said.

"You got that right," Leonard said. He cut into some eggs, ramps, and cheese with his fork.

Dominic passed me the dandelion salad and reached for the eggs Florentine. He wasn't interested in dinner conversation. He was only interested in the food.

Arabelle passed me the rolls and butter. "I've been meaning to ask, what are you doing with my ink and Rocco's paper? I remember you used to write stories. There was one about an emperor penguin visiting some guy in a loony bin, yeah, and there was one about a saber-toothed bunny. Are you turning Rocco's paper and my ink into something like that?"

"Not exactly."

"What exactly, then?" Leonard asked. He had moved on to some dandelion salad. The flower petals had been pushed to the side. I guess he was saving those for last.

"Yeah, what exactly?" Arabelle teased.

"I could say I'm just writing one word after another, but that's not completely right."

"Not to mention a cop-out," Dominic mumbled, not looking up from his plate.

"That's fair," I said. "Yes, I think that's fair."

"Well, what then, exactly?" Arabelle repeated, and there it was again, that sparkle.

"I'm writing about Wildcat."

"What about Wildcat?" Leonard asked.

"Yeah, what about Wildcat?" Arabelle added.

"I'm not getting out of this, am I?"

"Nope," Arabelle laughed.

"I'm just writing about being back. So much changed a long time ago, and then I left, and so much has changed recently, and now I'm back."

"And you're not on the hill anymore," Dominic interjected. He had put his fork down, but he didn't look my way. Instead, he looked out the window toward the river.

"That's true, Dominic. I'm not on the hill anymore."

AFTER DINNER

After dinner, I decided to take my thoughts and feelings down along the river and walk with the current. I put the mill behind me, the mill that had brought my family to the hill, the mill that was closed by my father and turned into an empty hulk, the mill that has become the cooperative for Rocco's mushroom transformations; Dougie, Terence, and Chéri's sassafras creations; and Floreandra's bee alchemy.

The moon hung full in the sky like one of Hotel Wildcat's well-seasoned dinner plates, and it lit my way so that I didn't trip over any rocks or driftwood, and then there were the chunks of concrete. I certainly didn't want to stumble over one of those.

Finally, I came to one of my favorite spots, the place where the creek comes down to the river. This confluence is much older than me, much older than Wildcat. It was here when the Seneca left and before they came. It was here after the glaciers left and before they came.

This confluence is here in ways all thoughts and feelings and experiences fail, and it's upon places like these that The Shadows endure.

OTTERS

I sat down on the shale bench that I like so much, the one that is covered with haircap moss. From there, I watched some shadows swim and dive and surface and swim some more. I was intrigued by the way they played, the coming together and parting and coming together again of their movement.

When I lived on the hill, I had never encountered these shadows, although I had discovered this place. Back then, I often stopped and sat on this soft green semicircle of a couch, but shadows like these were not there. At least I had not experienced them as such.

I have watched these shadows a few times since my return, and because they are a source of wonder, I asked Dominic, and he said, "Sounds like otters to me."

"Really?" I asked. "I used to sit down there all the time, but I never saw them."

"No, you wouldn't have. They were all trapped out in the eighteen hundreds."

"But now they're back?"

"Yeah, some people thought it was a good idea, so they collected otters from other places and brought them here."

"Like me?"

"Well, not exactly."

"What do you mean, not exactly?"

"Otters are native. You're not."

As I continued to watch their dark movements, an otter popped its head up from the creek and looked at me. I don't know what this otter was thinking, but I imagined it wondered if I belonged, and if I did, in what way.

While we continued looking, I at the otter and the otter at me, I remembered that this place was also a favorite of Carolyn's. We used to hold hands and walk along the river, and then we would come to this spot.

Often, we talked about my friend Dominic and her friend Arabelle, and we agreed that our two friends should get together, although they never did. Other times we would talk about the drawings Carolyn made that I liked so much, especially the one of a woman with a clock face who was pregnant with the sun, or about the stories I wrote. She really liked the one about a girl who became a tree and was cut down by her father.

Then, the otter barked and disappeared below the surface of the creek. I filled its absence with a memory, one of Carolyn and I making love just as the shadows of the hill and trees were coming down.

THE DAM

SOMETHING DIFFERENT

Back in Hotel Wildcat, I'm finished writing, but maybe not . . . because although I'm comfortable here in Wildcat, I'm not comfortable with myself. I know this because Arabelle and Dominic have said as much, especially Dominic. When they ask me questions, I don't have adequate answers. I'm not in tune with Wildcat's past like lifelong residents, at least the few who remain. These people are my friends, so if I'm going to stay, I need to deal with what happened here fifty years ago. And then there's Carolyn, the one with whom I have unfinished business.

To that end, I'll try writing something different, the story of the dam, the one that begins when my parents and I moved to the hill.

Classic Split Entry Raised Ranch

Moving to the hill was unremarkable because for us moving was routine. We would get settled in one place, and then my father would find a better job, or sometimes my mother didn't like where we were. I remember my father saying, "One place or another, work's work, but I only got one wife," and then my mother would smile in her it's-required-of-me sort of way. And sometimes my father's job was to close a failing business. He didn't like doing it, but he said those jobs always paid well.

The house we moved into was like all the others. It was a classic split entry raised ranch and was in one of those post–World War II housing developments, the ones that were planted and watered by the G.I. Bill and FHA loans. The basement had a two-car garage and a bedroom, a rec room, and bathroom/utility room. Upstairs was a kitchen, living/dining area, two bedrooms, and bathroom. The yard was a half acre of grass with a young Japanese maple in the front and a young blue spruce in the back.

I remember standing out front and feeling strange. It was all so new except it wasn't because I'd seen it all before: the curving streets that denied being a part of anyone's city block, the shoebox houses that were so much alike they clearly had the same parents, and the monoculture lawn that cried out for police protection when a dandelion bloomed its sunny, sexy bits.

It was quiet, spooky quiet, so quiet, in fact, that after the moving truck drove away, it felt like a cemetery, and then I thought that all post–World War II housing plans must be cemeteries, too. It wasn't a pleasant thought, this belief that I was born and still lived in a cemetery. I knew right then and there that I needed to find a way out. I needed an escape, so I went inside our new house and said, "Bye, Mom. Bye, Dad. I'm taking a walk."

"Where to?" Mom said.

"I think I'll walk down to Wildcat and look around."

"Sounds interesting. Be back for supper."

"What's for supper?" I asked.

"Fried ham and scalloped potatoes."

"What's for dessert?"

"Leftover angel food cake from your dad's birthday. We've got vanilla ice cream, too."

"Sounds great." And soon I was walking down Out Street, and I came to a hairpin turn, the one that marks the beginning of Wildcat. I saw a clapboard house on this side of the road and another clapboard house on the other side, and then I saw even more clapboard houses, all with front porches, some partially or completely enclosed and others completely open.

I turned off Out Street and onto Church Street and walked past more houses. Some had been remodeled a while back with Inselbric, the pre-1950s asphalt siding with a brick pattern stamped on it. And there was a real brick house next to the church.

I stopped for a moment to take in the architecture of the church. I thought it was a nice church with stairs in the middle that led to a basement entrance and then more stairs on the right that led up to a corner door, the one that opened into the sanctuary. The perfectly centered bell tower rose above the trees, an arrangement that brought the building back into symmetry. I wondered how the bell would sound when I heard it for the first time.

My next turn put me onto School Street, and I went past the place where I would learn to make sentences better fit my changing thoughts. The school was constructed from solid brick, a two-story fortress, the sort of architecture built back when America was new and wanted to reassure its children that it was here to stay, a real news photograph of a painting of a statue of someone in an encyclopedia.

EDUCATION

Early on in public school, I became good at finding this row, sitting in that seat, and looking out any number of windows. I was sure that my first day at the Wildcat school would be no different. I figured I had education down cold.

I wasn't too worried about making friends. We never lived anywhere long enough for serious friendships to develop, and at the time, I'd never had a *good* friend, so I didn't know what that felt like. I found it easy to roll with the changes my parents threw at me by adopting an easygoing attitude, and as for girls, I'd always been pretty gender-neutral. I thought people were people, right?

I have this grade school memory of walking home from school with a girl. We walked along together talking kid stuff. When we came to the girl's house, I went on by myself, and when I got to my house, my mother asked, "How was your day?"

"Okay, I guess," I answered. "I walked home with Suzie" (or Holly or Beth, I don't remember which girl).

"Oh, you did, did you?" my mother asked. I remember she put her hands on her hips and drew a crooked smile across her face. Obviously walking home with Suzie was a *big deal*, but I didn't know what was *soooo big* about it. Oh, I wasn't stupid. I knew it was because I had walked home with *a girl*, but I didn't think it ranked up there with not wearing pants.

But now, I was going to Wildcat's school, and after a few days, a girl in my science class got my attention. We didn't have traditional school desks where the seats were attached. Instead, we had tables and separate chairs, and this girl liked to tip back in her chair, a thing she did by balancing her chair on two legs and resting her elbows on the table behind.

What impressed me was her confidence. There was no fuss about it, and the teacher never said, "Hey, four on the floor. I don't need any cracked heads in here."

And it didn't stop there. I had trouble looking anywhere in the room but at her. It was like I could smell the sight of her, and then I would hold that smell up against me, soft, like she was a pillow, and I was a pillow, and someone had thrown us together on a bed just so.

It got so serious that the sight of her came home and moved in, and her image became the furniture of my mind. Sometimes she was a modern fifties couch: slim-tapered legs, sleek, with red velvet upholstery. Other times she was a Danish modern bed: dovetailed and teak-complected, with a low-profile silhouette.

HER NAME

"Arabelle Stept," the teacher said.

"Here."

"Boris Tomaszewski." No answer. "Boris, Boris Tomaczeski?"

"Oh, yeah, here."

"Dominic Vitali."

"Here."

"Patricia Widmer."

"Here."

"Carolyn Zalewski."

"Uh-huh."

"What?" the teacher asked.

"Present," Carolyn said.

NEW KID

I was the new kid. On weekday mornings, I'd walk down the hill from my house to school. After school, I'd take detours. Sometimes I'd cut left and other times I'd cut right across the hill and then find my way home. Sometimes I didn't feel much like going home, and if the weather was good, I'd walk along the river to the creek and then use game trails to find my way back for dinner. No matter how I went home, whether it was this way or that way or even down the river to the creek, I'd always stop somewhere and stand or sit or sometimes lie down. Sometimes I'd stop twice. Occasionally even more.

Looking back, it's clear I needed to decompress. All the students at school had grown up together and had intense relationships, many family-related, and although I was easygoing, I found that staying easygoing took effort. Back then, people called what I was doing "back to nature," and nowadays, people call it "Zen," but for me, walking and sitting in the woods recharged my battery. Besides, I wasn't in any hurry to return to the cemetery.

One day after school, instead of heading up Out Street and starting up the hill, I turned down toward the river, and as soon as the river came into view, a kid yelled in my general direction, "Hey, where you going?" I knew his name was Dominic because I'd heard it called during roll.

"My house," I said.

"You live the other way."

"Yes, I guess I do."

"So, how come you're going the wrong way?" Dominic asked.

"Uh, I'm not in a hurry to get there."

"No? Me neither."

Dominic and I stood there a bit without talking. He looked at me. I looked at him. We looked at each other until Dominic spit off to one side and said, "I think I'll come along."

"Okay."

"Good." And he spit again. I'd noticed a few days back that Dominic's back pocket had a circle worn into it, so his spitting came as no surprise. Then he spit a third time, and we started down to the river and walked with the current. "What do you think?" Dominic asked.

"Think about what?" I asked back.

"Wildcat?"

"Oh, Wildcat, right, it's okay. I've lived in different places. I like the woods and down by the creek."

"Me, too."

Dominic told me about his childhood adventures, and I told him about mine. His adventures were more interesting because his were about Wildcat and the trees he climbed, the hickories and oaks and maples, and the animals he knew, the deer and 'possums, and then there were the milk snakes, the ones that people thought were copperheads but weren't. My adventures came from someplace else, and although Dominic thought they were exotic in that distant sort of way, to me they felt less important because they weren't about Wildcat.

It didn't take long for me to ask Dominic about some of the people, and he told me about the teachers and the principal and about some of the characters who stumbled out of Hotel Wildcat. He had some good stories, and then he said, "Got a girlfriend?"

"No."

"Ever had a girlfriend?"

"Not really. You?"

"Not around here."

"Why not?" I wondered.

"Shit, man, it'd be wrong, you know."

"What do you mean?"

"They're like sisters. If I asked one out, they'd give me hell. I'd never hear the end of it. Forty years from now, I'd be in Hotel Wildcat knocking one back, and Arabelle, she'd be all wrinkly, and she'd yell across the room, 'Hey, Dominic, remember when you asked me out? Remember? You were such a fuckhead back then.' See what I'm saying?"

"I guess so."

"But you're the new kid, right? New is interesting, fresh meat."

"You're saying I should ask somebody out?"

"That's what I'm saying. So, who's it going to be?"

"I think Carolyn's interesting."

"Carolyn, huh? Interesting, huh? If you like that sort of thing."

"Maybe."

"Well, ask her out."

"Just like that?"

"Just like that."

WELL, ASK HER OUT

"Well, ask her out" was a lot easier said than done. At least it was for me.

Sure, I was okay around girls who were like me, ones who lived in new houses with two-car garages, whose moms only bought name brands, and whose dads golfed. Those were the girls I was used to. They were the ones I was expected to marry, although my parents never said so, at least not in so many words. Back then, it seemed as inevitable as a canned ham.

But Wildcat girls, and Carolyn was certainly one of those, were a whole different matter. From what I'd seen, Wildcat folks had one car, and it was parked outside. Oh, maybe there was another car, but it was missing a wheel, and the rotor disc was on a concrete block. It also seemed that Wildcat moms only went in for store brands. And the dads? Let's just say I saw a few deer, gutted and tied on the roofs of cars parked out in front of Wildcat homes.

Except maybe it wasn't so complicated. Perhaps "Well, ask her out" was as simple as choosing between canned ham or fresh venison, and when I looked at it that way, getting up some gumption was easier. Not easy, but easier.

The next afternoon, I took up position on the school's front steps, and when Carolyn came through the door, I was relieved to see she was by herself. Under one arm, she had her copy of *The Aquarian Gospel*, the book all Wildcat associated with Carolyn, a book that was a mystery to us all. She also had another book; one I hadn't seen before.

"What's that one about?" I asked.

"Which one?"

"Either one, really," I said falling in beside her. "How about the skinny one?"

"Oh, it's a kids' book."

"Okay."

"It's hard to describe."

"Okay, what's it called?"

That stopped Carolyn. She turned and held the book up, so I could see the cover. The title was *Topsy-Turvies: Pictures to Stretch the Imagination*. She didn't seem annoyed, but she didn't look very happy either. I think she was just waiting to find out what the hell was going on.

"Can I see?" I asked. I was trying to be as innocent as possible. And sincere.

"Sure," she said and handed me the book.

As it turned out, Carolyn wasn't kidding. When I opened *Topsy-Turvies*, I found it didn't have any words. I also didn't know what to make of the pictures, what with its elves dancing on ceilings and stairs leading to nowhere. I closed the book and read the author's name, Mitsumasa Anno. "Japanese, huh? It's fun to look at, but I'm pretty sure my mom wouldn't think so."

"So, your mom's no fun?" Carolyn poked.

"I guess so," I said and handed the book back.

As we started to walk, Carolyn led the way. I asked her questions, and she gave me answers. I wanted to know as much about Carolyn as possible, which really meant I liked the sound of her voice. Don't get me wrong, I was interested in her story, too, although she was a bit suspicious of me. She wondered why I was interested in Wildcat and, by association, in her.

Then we stopped, and Carolyn said, "This is my house."

Carolyn's house was only four feet off the street and cut into the hill. The front door went into the basement. Someone a long time ago had painted the door a battleship gray, and now the paint was peeling. The door had a window. At least I thought it was a window because someone had nailed plywood over it. And there was another window that someone, this time from the inside, had hung a white cloth across. It wasn't decorative. It was more like someone didn't want to be seen.

Above the basement were two more floors. The first floor was painted red a long time ago. It had a front porch, one that was mostly enclosed. A small portion of the porch had been left open, and that open space revealed a door. It seemed to me that this door wanted to be a front door, but as there were no stairs from the porch down to ground, it couldn't be that sort of door. It was just an escape hatch, a place for someone to go through to light up a cigarette or jump from to get away.

The second floor was also painted red. It had two small, double-hung windows, ones that peered out toward the river. The windows were like eyes, but the house's other features were hidden behind the porch, and as I stood there taking it all in, I decided the house was really peeking over the porch. Without that porch, the house didn't have the courage to look out at the world at all.

"This was fun," I said. "Mind if I wait for you tomorrow? It's kind of on my way."

"If you want." Then, Carolyn turned away. I thought I caught a hint of a smile before she disappeared through her basement door. Of course, it's possible I only saw what I wanted to see. Maybe Carolyn didn't smile at all. But then again . . .

WALKS

That's when I began waiting for Carolyn after school. She didn't seem to mind, and the sight of her coming through the school's door changed me, and I was happy for what was going on.

Our first walks went straight from the school to her house, but soon we took more indirect routes. We'd make a figure S by starting on School Street, and then we'd cut back on Church Street, and once we passed the church, we'd turn onto White Damp Way and end up at Carolyn's house.

It didn't take long for Carolyn and me to change our route even more. Sometimes, we headed up Out Street and cut left or right across the hill. And then a bit later, we changed our route again. This time we headed down Out Street to the river before coming to the creek, where we stopped at the shale bench, the one covered with haircap moss.

Back then, there were no dark movements of otters coming together and parting and coming together again. We didn't know that the last otter had been trapped before we were born and its cold, hard body taken from the creek. How were we to know? It's not something people talked about.

HOLDING HANDS

During the time of our exploration, Carolyn and I shared the same English class. Our teacher was not like our other teachers, and as such, he had our attention. He was born and raised on the other side of the river, had gone to college to escape killing and being killed, and then took a job teaching English at the school.

One day he taught us about haiku. He told us that poetry didn't need to rhyme, which was news to us, and then he told us a lot more that we didn't fully understand. He said poetry didn't need to have a clapped-out rhythm. He told us that poetry only had to have a few lines, although he knew a poem without any words, just a title. He told us that haiku was poetry that had five syllables in the first line, seven syllables in the second line, and five in the third line. And then he said that counting syllables was English teacher bullshit. Yes, he blushed a bit, and we respected him for the cursing and even more for the blushing. He went on to say that in Japan, poets didn't count actual syllables; in Japan, poets only accented the first line twice, the second line three times, and the third twice more.

He wanted us to know that traditional Japanese haiku poets made reference to a season—summer, fall, winter, spring—and that they created a shift in image, meaning, or perspective somewhere in the poem, often near the end of the second line. But he made it clear that those were traditional Japanese poets, and we were not traditional Japanese poets. No, we were Wildcat poets, and then he directed us to write our own haiku.

So, I did, and when I'd finished my very first one, I passed it to Carolyn.

kneeling under a
flowering apple: a morel,
fingers woven tight

BANG

THE MINE

EXPLODED

THE MINE EXPLOSION

Carolyn and I were in English class when the mine exploded. We felt the explosion as much as we heard it. The wood floors and the brick walls of the school flexed. The milk glass globes on their light chains swayed. Our desks rattled.

Our English teacher yelled, "WHAT THE..." And then all was silent. We watched to see what he would do. Then, we looked at each other. Maybe the expression on our faces might tell us something.

Finally, after collecting himself, our teacher said with an authority born of the moment, "Earthquake. Get under your desks. That's what they do in California."

Because he was our teacher, we got under our desks. Who were we to argue? We'd never been to California.

Time passed at the speed of breath. Those of us who were anxious breathed rapidly, and time bolted out, crackling our edges. Those of us, including me, who were calm slowed our breathing, and time flowed out, softening our edges.

I looked about and noticed that our English teacher wasn't under his desk. He stood in front of us, arms crossed. I thought he was looking out the window, although I couldn't be sure. After all, I was sitting under my desk, and from that vantage, I couldn't follow his line of sight. All the same, I thought he was looking at the river.

I thought this because I'd been to the river many times, and when I was there, I always felt my troubles pulled from me and carried downstream. I knew that my teacher had been born and raised on the other side of the river, and I was sure that, like me, he had been to the river and that the river worked on him in the same extraordinary way.

"All teachers and students are to leave the building immediately and report to the parking lot," the public address speaker barked. "Students, stay with your teachers. Teachers, take your roll books. Once we are all assembled in the parking lot, teachers, take attendance."

We got out from under our desks and up off the floor and began to shuffle toward the door. Carolyn and I fell together, and we all followed our English teacher into the hall, down the stairs, and out to the parking lot. Our English teacher was the good shepherd, *baa*, we were his precious sheep, *baa, baa*, and soon we were together in our asphalt pasture, *baa, baa, baa*.

After he took roll, our teacher stood quietly but looked troubled. I felt maybe he was worried about the people he knew across the river, wondering if they were safe or if he could find his way back to them. It could be he just realized that we were not in California. Once again, I had no way of knowing, but then he turned and looked back to the river, and although I could no longer see his expression, his unease spread to all of us.

"Students, I have some very bad news," the principal

said. She was wearing her usual checked skirt and floral blouse, but now she also had a bullhorn. "There has been an explosion in the mine. I know many of you have fathers or other relatives or friends who work there. I know that mine accidents are something we all worry about every day. We never know when one may happen, but now one has, and all we can do is wait for information. I don't know how bad the accident was or if any of the miners were hurt. I wish I knew more, but I don't, and all we can do is pray.

"I've decided that, in light of what has happened, it would be foolish to continue the school day. People at home may need you. You may need them. And with that in mind, you may leave when I'm finished talking if there is someone at home to greet you, or if you are old enough to take care of yourself. For those of you who prefer to stay here, of course, you are welcome, and your teachers are staying to care for you. We will be here for you until you can be with your loved ones.

"I'm so sorry to tell you this tragic news, but since we all heard and felt the explosion, there was no reason not to tell you. God bless and protect us all.

"And now, at this time, those who are ready to return home may do so. Those who are staying may follow your teacher inside."

When the principal was finished, I felt Carolyn's fingers entwined with mine. I wasn't aware that we were holding hands. Then I was.

CAROLYN'S MOM

I walked Carolyn home. We walked straight there. We didn't go up and across the hill. We didn't go down to the river and then to the creek. We held hands along the way.

When we got to her house, Carolyn opened the door and led me inside. I had not been inside her house before. She hadn't been interested in me going inside, but now the mine had exploded, and things had changed.

The basement was dark and musty, and there were objects stacked here and there, shadows on top of shadows. I couldn't put names to anything, but it was clear that molds and mildews had found this place: a confederation of rot.

Carolyn led me up some wooden stairs. They were steep and rickety, and the treads were thin. I imagined that some-day someone would break through. I didn't think it would be me in my canvas tennis shoes. No, it would be someone in heavy boots, body-blown by work, filled with a shot and a beer, maybe more than one.

Once on the first floor, Carolyn and I walked into the kitchen. Florescent light mixed with daylight and cigarette smoke, a sickly yellow. It wasn't amber. It wasn't canary. And it wasn't goldenrod. It was sickly. Dishes and glasses were piled in the sink. A cast-iron skillet sat on an old four-burner gas stove. It wore the crust of many meals.

"Mom, this is the new kid."

"Hi, Mister New Kid," Carolyn's mom said. Her tone was one I hadn't heard before. I could tell we weren't going to hit it off, at least not at first, but she wasn't going to kick me out either.

"The principal told us to go home," Carolyn said. She sat down next to her mom at the aluminum-framed, Formica-topped kitchen table. It was yellow, too. Sickly.

Her mom didn't answer right off. She took a long drag on her cigarette and then nothing. I waited for her to exhale, for the smoke to rush out and join the haze. It seemed like a long time before she exhaled, and it seemed like nothing could happen until she did. Apparently, Carolyn's mom could stop time by smoking a cigarette.

After she exhaled, Carolyn's mom kicked an aluminum-framed, vinyl-upholstered chair out from the table. "Sit down, Mister New Kid." She took another long drag on her cigarette and crushed the butt in a jar lid filled with ashes and other butts. "I's glad your brother don't work in that mine. I's glad when he got that job at the mill. That mine, I don't want to talk about it."

Through the smoke, I could see that Carolyn's mom was wearing a faded, floral housedress. The flowers were almost gone. The threads, too.

Her face was a battleground. Life had engraved deep furrows, but the underlying fat was pushing back.

She seemed to be comfortable on her kitchen chair in the way people are comfortable when they don't plan on going anywhere. Ever.

Then, Carolyn, her mother, and I heard the basement door open, and right after that, we heard it slam. We listened to the sound of heavy work boots coming up the basement steps. And we waited, but I didn't know what for.

CAROLYN'S BROTHER

A man came into the kitchen. He didn't look at Carolyn. He didn't look at her mother. And he certainly didn't look at me.

I couldn't tell how old he was. At first, I thought he was young, maybe two years older than Carolyn, five at the most. But his face was puffy, especially under his eyes. His complexion was swarthy, but probably not the color he was born with. No, it was like the dirt of his life had been ground in. He had a full-facial grime tattoo.

"Shut the mill down," the man said.

"Oh," Carolyn's mother said.

"The principal sent us home because of the accident. Is that why you're home?" Carolyn asked.

"Maybe. Shit, I don't know." He looked lost, and then he opened the battered refrigerator. He grabbed a bottle of beer and popped off the cap with his belt buckle.

"This is the new kid," Carolyn said.

For the first time, the man tried to focus. When he was done, he turned, spit in the sink, took a swig of beer, wiped his mouth on his sleeve, and said, "Uh-huh." Then, he stuck out his hand. There wasn't much space between us in the small kitchen. "Charles."

I touched his rough, grubby hand with my soft, smooth hand. That's all it took. We were done. I was New Kid. He was Charles, Carolyn's brother.

WHAT CHARLES KNEW

"Damn, Charles, you must know something," Carolyn half-pleaded. Her other half was pissed.

But the Charles I saw wasn't in any hurry. He looked at his mom, and she smiled back, sort of, and she lit up another cigarette. Then, he turned and spit in the sink, again. Took a pull on his bottle, again. Wiped his mouth on his sleeve, again. Looked my way, but not because he was interested, and then he looked down at the floor and said, "Mine's been on reduced shift, just like us. Weren't many in there. Heard it was gas. White damp. Just a matter of time."

"Was anybody hurt?" Carolyn asked.

"Three."

"Three?" Carolyn pleaded.

"Three."

"Who? How bad?" Now, Carolyn was pissed.

"Well . . ." and Charles stopped to spit in the sink. Took a swig. Wiped his mouth. "Three's dead."

"Who?" Carolyn pleaded, again.

"Don't matter. Dead's dead."

"Damn, Charles, *who*?" Now, Carolyn was pissed, again.

"Some guy named Abernathy, he's dead. And another guy named Valentin, he's dead, too. And Luigi."

"Dominic's Luigi?"

"Dead."

"*Shit*." And then Carolyn drew her arms about her and got really small.

As for me, I was on the outside looking in. I had no business saying anything and leaving would have been rude, so I just sat there, out of place, a clean dish in the sink.

Carolyn's mom took another drag on her cigarette, and, again, nothing. Time stopped, again. It was like the world held its breath. No drip came from the faucet. A spider quit spinning, and a fly stopped buzzing against the greasy window glass.

But before Carolyn's mom could exhale, Charles spit, took a swig, wiped his mouth, and looked my way, again, but this time he didn't look at the floor. This time he kept his eyes on me and said, "Kill us one way or another."

And only then did Carolyn's mom send a long, slow stream of smoke out into the sickly yellow air.

FOR DOMINIC

shadow on shadow,
pussy willows by the creek,
a fallen egg, crack

THE FUNERAL

Wildcat became very sad. We didn't know there was more sadness to come. We all waited for the calm after the storm. No one waits for the storm after the storm. And there was the anger.

The bodies of the ones who entered the mine that morning, Abernathy and Valentin and Dominic's older brother Luigi, were brought to the church.

Coffins needed to be constructed, so men from the church got together. The boxes were made quickly and with skill. The wood was chestnut and came from an abandoned outbuilding. It had been very old, aged in the way things become when no one remembers.

All of Wildcat attended the funeral as did a few from the hill. It was a cool day. My father put on a suit, and my mother wore a coat over her dress. I put on a shirt and tie with a blue blazer, and then we started down from the hill and found ourselves a portion of open pew. Soon, the church was full with people standing along the sides and in the back. Only the middle aisle was left open.

I saw the back of Carolyn's head. She was sitting next to her mother, and Charles was on the other side. I hoped that she would turn around and see me. I thought that seeing her face would bring at least a bit of the change I liked so much, the one that came when I saw her come through the door after school, but she didn't turn around.

71

The coffins were placed at the front of the church, in between the pews and the altar. One coffin was in the center. Whoever came down the aisle would go around it. A second coffin was on the left, and the third one was on the right. I wondered who was in each coffin. Were Luigi's remains in the center coffin or was it someone else? There was no way for me to know.

"The Lord be with you," a man said from behind the altar.

"And also with you," we responded.

I hadn't been inside the church, and I was surprised that the man behind the altar had on his buffalo coat. It was the red and black plaid wool coat worn by many Wildcat men, but I expected to see someone draped in a minister's robe and stole. Apparently, the church didn't have a minister, maybe he had left, or the congregation couldn't afford one. I didn't know why the church didn't have a minister, but I learned during the funeral that it didn't seem to matter.

"Out of the depths I cry unto thee," we sang.

Then, the man in the buffalo coat said a prayer, we sang some more, and there were some Bible readings. After that, the same man told us all about "this veil of tears" and "the resurrection of the dead" and "everybody meeting up again in heaven." I wondered about all that. I got the veil of tears part, but I didn't know about the resurrection and the meeting in heaven part. I supposed I'd just have to wait and see.

After the funeral was over, several men carried the coffins down the center aisle and put them on the beds of three pickup trucks waiting outside. This seemed odd to me, but when I thought about it, I realized that in all my wanderings about Wildcat, I'd never come across a cemetery. The church didn't have a cemetery nor was there one anywhere around town, at least not within walking distance.

I stood and waited in front of the church and watched as the three pickup trucks took Abernathy, Valentin, and Luigi down Church Street to Out Street.

When my parents and I went outside, I looked for Carolyn. I spotted her on the other side of Church Street. Her mother and Charles were not with her. Instead, she was with Dominic. And she was crying.

THE NEXT DAY

The next day I waited for Carolyn after school, and when I saw her, she wasn't by herself. She was with Dominic, and instead of me falling in beside her, Carolyn and Dominic stopped in front of me.

The three of us stood for a bit. We were nervous, didn't make much eye contact, and waited for someone to speak. We all felt uncomfortable in our own ways for our own reasons until this word came out of my mouth, "Sorry."

"Yeah," Dominic said.

"I never met him," I said.

"No, you didn't."

"How much older was he?" I asked.

"Seven, maybe eight years. Depends."

"I don't have brothers and sisters. Were you close?" I asked.

"Don't know about close. He was older. My dad worked in the mine, but his lungs got bad, so Luigi, he went to work."

Carolyn was looking at Dominic, her eyes narrowed, her gaze steady. I had not seen Carolyn this way before. She didn't look sad, and she didn't look my way.

"I got to get home," Dominic continued.

"How about let's walk to your house together," I reacted. "You'd like that, Carolyn, right?"

Carolyn turned and gave me a short burst of her steady gaze and then turned back to Dominic.

"Thanks, but I'll head home. You two just do what you do." And with that, Dominic walked away. He headed deeper into Wildcat. He didn't go in the direction of Out Street, and he didn't go toward the river or Hotel Wildcat or the mill. Instead, he went in a different direction.

SORRY

Carolyn and I walked silently along Church Street to Out Street and down between Hotel Wildcat and the mill. On Wildcat Beach, we joined hands and walked between the dairy and the river down to the creek. We rested on the bench covered with its community of haircap moss.

"I like this place," I said.

"I know," Carolyn said.

"I'm so sorry," I said.

She looked into my eyes.

I kissed her hard. She kissed me wet.

CLOSED

After the accident, the mine was closed. This wasn't the first time, so no one was surprised.

I learned that Wildcat people were used to hard times and were self-sufficient in ways I didn't know. Gardening and canning. Hunting and smoking. Foraging. There was always a pile where something could be found and put to use. Great pride was taken in "making do."

But rent was still owed, and coffee and flour were not free. Bullets were cheap, but not free.

And no one predicted that, when the mine closed this time, it was closed for good.

MAY DAY

Leaves came out on the trees: oaks and red maples, chestnuts and hickories, sassafras and, of course, pussy willows along the creek.

Cherries and tulips bloomed. Morels came up under old apple trees. Chicken of the woods fruited from oaks. Oyster mushrooms sprouted on stumps.

Carolyn took me ramp hunting. It was the first time for me. We walked out across the hill together, but this time, instead of heading down the river toward the creek, we went up the river.

It was one of those glorious days where a light breeze brought a potpourri of flower scent, and the sun washed the shadows from the hill. Every songbird was in full throat, warming up their instruments for their symphony of babel. The insects were in perfect riot.

"Are we going to a favorite spot?" I asked after we walked about a half hour.

"Not exactly."

"Where, then?"

"We're going past where I've found them before. Maybe there'll be some. Maybe someone will have beat us to them. Maybe they haven't come up yet. Maybe they won't come up at all this year."

"So, you're not sure?"

"Maybe you're kind of dumb. Maybe," Carolyn said and smiled. After seeing her with her family, I understood why Carolyn was always so direct, none of the sugarcoating my parents traded in, and certainly none of the meaningful silence.

As we continued on, Carolyn told me that ramps loved

shade and ramps loved damp. Good places were found just below springs that kept the ground moist all summer long—damp, but not soggy.

She also said that ramps were best kept in a paper grocery bag. She had folded the one she had brought in the middle and carried it in her left hand so that she could join her right hand with mine. When the trail was wide enough, we continued along holding hands, but sometimes the trail was little more than a game trail, and sometimes we had to climb or descend in such a way that holding hands compromised our balance. On these occasions, Carolyn dropped my hand and took the lead. After all, these were her woods, and as for me, well, I was just a blow-in.

After about an hour, we went up and across a little rise and then down an embankment, and there we found a considerable patch of ramps. To me, they looked like lilies of the valley. I had learned about lilies of the valley from my mother. She had really liked this flower, but she had also taught me that they were poisonous. I wondered if there were other connections between my mother and Carolyn, but then I decided to stop thinking about my mother. I kept my mother to myself. After all, these were not my mother's woods; they were Carolyn's.

After I stopped thinking about my mother, Carolyn pulled a single-blade, six-inch jackknife from her pocket. She used her short thumbnail to pry up the blade, and although this was an old knife, Carolyn had kept the blade clean and sharp. I had never seen a knife blade whose shape had been altered by constant honing. That blade told me something about Carolyn that I didn't know. Clearly, Carolyn took good care of what was important. I didn't know if I was important. I wondered if I'd find out.

I also figured I'd better make myself useful, so I pulled out my standard-issue pocketknife and pried it open.

Carolyn took one look at the exposed blade and said, "Nah, put it back."

"What?"

"Put it back."

"But I'd like to help." I really did.

"Not with that."

"Why not?" I wondered.

"Dull."

"Okay, but it'll still work." I was sure it would.

"Okay, but it won't. You'll hurt the ramps, and then they'll go away."

"Uh . . ."

"Uh, my ass. First, you don't dig ramps. They're not onions, and they're not garlic. You leave the bulbs in the ground so that they send up nice leaves next spring. And you only trim off one leaf, not two and definitely not all of them. You only cut off one so that the others can feed the bulb, and then more leaves come up next year."

"I had no idea."

"And that's why you're the new kid," she smiled.

DEVOTION

C arolyn cut the ramps. Then, she handed them to me, and I gently laid each leaf in the grocery bag, the one she had brought for such purposes.

When she cut enough leaves to fill about a quarter of the bag—this patch was sizable—she stopped cutting, closed her knife, and led me to a spot along the embankment. There we sat down.

Reaching inside the bag, Carolyn pulled out a ramp. "Open up. Stick out your tongue."

I opened my mouth, and Carolyn gently laid the ramp on my tongue. At first, I smelled something almost garlicky, but only almost, and then I closed my mouth and slowly chewed. There was a pungency mixed with sweetness, and while I chewed, the pungency dissipated a little, leaving a bit more sweetness, but only a little. Finally, after the juice and fibers mixed with my saliva, I swallowed: ramps.

Following her lead, I reached into the bag and pulled out another ramp. Carolyn opened her mouth, and I gently laid the leaf on her tongue. She let it lie for a moment. Then, her lips puckered and closed, and she began to chew ever so slowly. She was in no hurry.

Over time, Carolyn had nurtured an affinity with these plants. She had waited a year, the absence growing, her desire building, and now Carolyn had taken the tulip-shaped blade inside, the ramp releasing its essence, her devotion rewarded.

So Much

Carolyn and I made desperate love upon the fertile embankment, strewn with our clothing, above the voluptuous ramps.

Back in Wildcat

After making love, Carolyn and I returned to Wildcat. She held my hand, and I held her paper grocery bag, the one filled with fresh-cut ramps. The sun was no longer above Wildcat. It had once been high in the sky, but now it hung down over the river, bright, its light cutting around the shadows deepening up the hill.

When we came to Carolyn's house, she opened the basement door, and I followed her into the gloom. Carolyn didn't lead me through her basement much, but when she did, I felt as if the dust were lying in wait. It was like the dust didn't want me to leave, the Dominion of Dust, and although the borders were open, I felt they might unexpectedly shut like a catacomb door.

Once upstairs, Carolyn and I saw Charles sitting at the kitchen table. He had built a wall of beer bottles in front of him.

"Where's Mom?" Carolyn asked.

Before answering, Charles took a swig of beer and wiped his mouth on his sleeve. He reached for a cigarette, the one smoldering in the ashtray, put the butt to his lips, took a long drag, and exhaled. "Out."

"Uh-huh," Carolyn replied, and I looked for some expression in her eyes. Nothing.

"Bought you two a bottle of wine." Charles kicked out a chair for Carolyn. "Sit down. We'll celebrate," and he closed his eyes and took another long drag on that cigarette, the one fast becoming almost as important to Charles as his beer bottle—almost.

After Carolyn sat down next to Charles, I pulled out a chair across from him and sat down. We waited while Charles sat and held the cigarette smoke. Up to now, I had not seen a resemblance between Charles and his mother, but now something had changed, and I wondered if it might be the cigarette smoke working deep inside him.

Finally, Charles ever so slowly exhaled, and his eyes, expressionless, now focused on me. "Open it and serve the lady."

Who was I to argue? After all, I was the new kid, so I did as I was told and screwed the cap off the wine bottle, but unfortunately, I didn't know what to do next. Charles had said "serve the lady," but there were no glasses, and it wasn't my place to rummage about or even ask, "Where are the glasses?" so I just held the open bottle limply in my hand.

"Come on now, new kid, take a swig and then give your lady the bottle."

I did as I was told and put the bottle to my lips. First came a thick sweetness and then the sharp acid. The taste was new to me. I found it unpleasant, but I smiled and then handed the bottle to Carolyn.

I watched as Carolyn tipped the bottle back. Her lips puckered, and she pulled a serious swig. It was not the sort of tentative sip I had taken. Clearly, Carolyn was well acquainted with this bottle. I was curious to see if the bottle would meet her expectations. As for me, I didn't know what to expect, but I hoped that the bottle wouldn't disappoint Carolyn.

Without looking my way, Carolyn reached and set the bottle in front of me, and then Charles said, "White port. Cheap. Effective. Sweet, too. Goes right to your head and then some. Drink up, you two. Then, I want to hear what's going on."

Again, I did as I was told and took another sip, only this time I got enough that it would be clear that I had swallowed. I didn't want Carolyn, or Charles for that matter, to think I didn't appreciate being included.

After I handed the bottle back to Carolyn, she took another swig, and then Charles took a drag on his cigarette.

He held the smoke and exhaled and took a swig of beer and wiped his mouth on his sleeve, which all was preliminary to returning to the topic at hand.

"Well now, what's going on with you two?" He looked directly at me when he said "you two."

I was in no position to answer, but Carolyn sure was. "Ah, lay off him, Charles. He's my friend, that's all."

"Friend? And friend can't speak for himself?"

"Friend don't have to speak for himself if friend don't want to. Friend's my friend, and any brother of mine who says differently's an asswipe."

Carolyn's words made Charles look away from me and back to his beer. Drag. Hold. Exhale. Swig. Wipe. And then Charles looked directly at his sister and said, "Asswipe, huh? I'll have to think on that some. But here's what I'm wondering. Now tell me the truth, friend's lady, you two got it on yet?"

"None of your damn business, asswipe."

"I'll take that as a yes."

"Asswipe."

"S'pose I had it coming."

"Asswipe."

And then we were quiet. I sipped. Carolyn swigged. Charles opened a new bottle and knocked back the contents until Carolyn said, "So, asswipe, what is it *you're* celebrating?"

A Mean Dog's Eye

From what I'd seen of Charles, he wasn't the emotional type. Oh, he had emotions, but nothing much seeped through the grime and the attitude and the beer.

I could see the sort of intelligence in Charles that I'd seen in a mean dog's eye as it lay on a front porch watching me. The dog didn't bark. The dog didn't move, and as I walked past, I thought that the dog was going back to sleep, but something also told me that the dog's eye was following me. A mean dog's eye.

"Well?" Carolyn probed.

Nothing.

"Well, Charles?" Carolyn could be sarcastic, too.

Then, we waited and waited some more for the answer to Carolyn's question, "What is it *you're* celebrating?" We waited while Charles drained the last half of his current bottle. We waited while Charles wiped his mouth on his sleeve, and then, and only then, did Charles speak—"Laid off"—punctuated by opening another bottle.

"Laid off?" Carolyn asked.

"Fired."

"Uh, which one?" Carolyn was incredulous.

Lacking a better idea, Carolyn and I watched Charles kill the first half of the bottle and then kill the second half, which led to him opening another bottle before wiping his mouth on his sleeve and saying, "Mill's closed."

"I don't understand," Carolyn said, and I had to admit I didn't either. "The mill's closed, and you're laid off, but then you said you're fired."

"Mine's shut for good. Mill's been shut for good. Asswipe's got nowhere to work. Wildcat's been fucked. That *what* you want to know?"

"Shit," Carolyn said.

"Shit? You got that right."

"Shit . . . What're you going to do, Charles?" Carolyn's incredulity had turned to fear.

Charles went back to his cigarette, took a long drag, and slowly exhaled. He looked at his beer bottle, and then put the bottle to his lips and drained the entire bottle. "I'm thinking on that, sis. Your asswipe brother is thinking on that. And you, new kid, you might want to think on it, too." When Charles said, "new kid," he didn't look at me, but he didn't need to. Like I said, a mean dog's eye.

WHAT CHARLES WILL DO

Later, Carolyn and I stood outside her house. Charles had upset Carolyn, and I must admit he'd upset me, too, not so much with what he said, but with what he didn't.

"What do you think Charles is going to do?" I asked Carolyn.

"I don't know. But I'm worried."

"Do you think he'll take a job somewhere else and move away? Do you think you and your mom will go with him?"

"No, I don't think he'll move away," Carolyn said. Her eyes were looking in the direction of the river, but I felt they were really focused inside.

"Okay, but what do you think he'll do? After all, he is your brother, and he is the one who has a job. At least he did."

"Oh, he'll probably smoke cigarettes like my mom, but he'll also drink like my dad."

"But he already drinks."

"Not like my dad."

TIP OF THE ICEBERG

The end of the school year was nearing for Carolyn and me, and Dominic quit coming to school much. He'd show up on this day and, then again, a few days later, but he clearly had lost interest in the end of school.

One day while I was waiting after school for Carolyn, I saw Dominic coming down the street. He had a crowbar with him, and he was headed against the river.

I waited to see if he would turn toward the school, but he didn't, and when it was clear he wouldn't be coming my way, I called out, "Hey, Dominic, where're you going?"

I know he heard me because he stopped. He didn't turn my way. He didn't call back. He just stopped.

After a few moments, he lifted the crowbar off his shoulder and raised it to the merciless sun.

Then, Dominic lowered the crowbar onto his shoulder and started walking again, only this time I thought his pace had quickened, his gait more determined.

I've thought a lot about this image of Dominic, the one he left in my mind so long ago. I thought he was trying to tell me something, but at the time, I didn't know what it was.

Sometimes a leaf just floats on the surface, but other times, well, this was one of those other times.

THE BELL

School ended for the year on Wednesday, and the next morning the large bell in the church started ringing: *bong bong bong bong bong bong bong.*

I was still in bed, as it was very early, and the sun was still tucked behind the hill. Soon, the sun would make its entrance. It would first peek over the hill, and then, it would begin its triumphant climb over Wildcat, but now I lay in bed waking up to the deep, rhythmic resonance coming up the hill.

Of course, it wasn't Sunday, and the ringing was not the calmly paced Sunday claps that called Wildcat to church. Instead, the ringing was quick and insistent. It was like a dog that is running, but the dog's back legs are a bit ahead of its front legs, so that the dog is always in danger of tripping over itself. Whoever was ringing the church bell was in some sort of hurry.

I was curious, so I got out of bed and rubbed the sleep from my eyes. I had gone to bed in a T-shirt and underwear. The night had been hot and humid, and the morning was bringing more of the same, so I put on a pair of jeans, stuck my feet in some tennis shoes, and headed out toward the kitchen. My mother and father were waiting. They were dressed and ready for the day, as was their rule. My mother's hair was perfect, as if she hadn't slept at all. My father wore gray slacks with a white shirt and a blue and gold striped tie. My mother wore white capris and a rose-checked crinkle blouse.

Bong bong bong.

"What's going on?" I asked.

"I don't know," my dad said. He looked concerned. My mother didn't show anything.

"Well, *something's* going on," I said.

"Either that or somebody's gone a bit crazy," my dad said. "It's too early for work, but I think I'll go down anyway and see what's what."

Although the mill was closed, which is to say the production line had been shut down, my father still worked there. I'm not sure why he still worked there. I just knew that he did.

Bong bong bong, and my mother and I followed my father out the door and into the shy early morning light.

THE FIRE

People came from Wildcat and stood in front of the mill. A few other people came down the hill and stood with them. My parents and I were some of those.

As school was out for the year, many of my classmates were standing among the growing crowd, some here, some over there. I looked for Carolyn, and at first, I didn't see her, but then there she was, standing in front of the store. I waved, and she began to move my way. I didn't see Carolyn's mother, and I didn't see Charles. Carolyn appeared to be by herself, at least until she made her way to me. Then, she and I were standing between Hotel Wildcat and the mill.

I joined hands with Carolyn, and we watched as smoke came from under the mill's door, not the shop door but the office door.

"By yourself?" I asked Carolyn.

"Uh-huh."

"Your mom at home?"

"Uh-huh."

"Charles?"

"Don't know."

Carolyn and I stood with people mostly from Wildcat but also some from the hill. We watched as three pickups turned off Church Street onto Out Street and came down to a spot between the river and the mill. They were the same pickups that, after the funeral, had taken away the coffins, the ones that contained Abernathy and Valentin and Luigi, Dominic's older brother. When the pickups stopped, the drivers got out. The sun was fully resplendent above the hill. Today, there was no need for buffalo coats.

My father left my mother with the crowd and went over to talk with the men. I couldn't hear what they were saying, but first my father talked, and the men nodded, and then the men talked, and my father nodded. Whatever was said seemed to do the trick because right after my father nodded, the men trotted to the back of their pickups and dropped the tailgates. Each grabbed a two-inch hose and headed to the river. The hoses were attached to portable pumps driven by gasoline engines.

After tossing the free ends of their hoses into the river, the men returned to their pickups and started up their pumps. Soon, they had three pressurized fire hoses ready to go.

As the three men approached the mill, a fourth man, a balding old man of the woods wearing a twisted gray beard, walked up to the mill office door. He grabbed the door handle and pulled the door open.

Smoke from behind the door billowed out. The smoke didn't seem to want to be in the building anymore, what with more smoke being born all the time. Once the smoke came outside, it swallowed the old man.

Everyone in the crowd was concerned about the old man. We were worried the smoke would be too much for him. We didn't want the old man to be overcome, and maybe he would be unable to breathe. We didn't express these concerns to each other, but we were all individually concerned just the same. Looking back, it was as if we were staring into our own uncertain future, a time when nothing would ever be right again. What were we to do?

Trying to be helpful, we stepped back to allow the men with the hoses to start sending steady streams of water into the mill. In very little time, the water from the river knocked down the smoke, and we in the crowd could see the old man sitting on the ground, coughing, rubbing his eyes, and then coughing some more.

A few Wildcat women attended to the old man while the men with the hoses went into the mill to finish putting out the fire. It was not difficult work because it turned out there was much more smoke than fire.

That's when Carolyn and I heard Dominic's voice behind us, "I'll be damned, someone busted the lock. What's up with that?"

We turned to find Dominic behind us. He shrugged.

I shook my head, and Carolyn didn't react at all.

THE DAM

The dam was built after someone burrowed into the hill, and the mine was born. The dam was built after someone fired up the coal to smelt iron, and the mill was born. The dam was built after someone formed the iron into rails, and the railroad was born.

But the dam, well, it was called a dam, but really the dam was no Aswan High and no Hoover and certainly no Jinping. The dam didn't control floods. It didn't generate power. It didn't help irrigate. It didn't store water, and it didn't even do much for recreation.

In fact, the dam didn't even look like a dam. It really was just a wall for the river to flow over, and if you didn't know that the swell in the river was caused by the dam, you wouldn't even know it was there. Oh, you didn't want to go canoeing and like a log wash over the thing. No, that never ended well.

And if you asked around, a lot of people in Wildcat knew someone who knew someone who didn't respect the current and undertow created by the dam. A lot of people knew someone who knew someone who one day was warm and sparkle-eyed, and the next day was pulled from the river cold and fish-eyed.

That being said, the dam was built because the Army Corps of Engineers had a dream of coal-filled barges moving up and down the river, but the corps had a problem: the river's water level quite naturally dropped in late summer and early fall. In fact, there were places that became so shallow that if you lifted your skirts or rolled up your pants, you could walk from Wildcat across the river and back.

And since the Army Corps of Engineers was, after all, an army, they weren't planning on taking no for an answer from this or any other kind of river, so they up and built the dam. Soon, no more dredging. Soon, no more late summer, early fall shallows, just one coal barge in the dam's lock after another, all the other barges waiting in a line that stretched from the northern horizon to the southern.

One time I asked Dominic, "Hey, how come there's a dam here?"

"What?" Dominic asked back.

"Well, I know they built it to move coal barges, but the mine's just up from the mill. It's not like the mill needs any of the coal from all those barges."

And then Dominic answered my question with a question: "Now, let me get this straight, you think anyone gives a fuck about Wildcat?"

WHAT CHARLES DID

We thought we'd seen all there was to see. We had started out as the sun rose to its rightful place above Wildcat. We had stood between Hotel Wildcat and the mill and seen the fire that led to the insistent ringing of the church's bell. We had watched smoke engulf an old man and then the river's water beat back the smoke. The fire was now out, and we began to think about doing something else.

I looked at Carolyn. She looked at me. I thought she looked beautiful with her large glasses magnifying her sky-blue eyes. She generally put on very little makeup, and this morning she wore none at all. It suited her.

I squeezed her hand and said, "Why don't..."

But I was interrupted by the sound of an engine starting up. It sounded like it was coming from somewhere behind the mill. It didn't sound like a car or a truck. It seemed to be a smaller engine, maybe a lawn mower, but the sound was a little more serious, maybe an outboard engine, the sort used for powering a small boat.

We stopped thinking about other things and turned our attention to the sound. There was no reason for us to do this. The sound of a small engine was hardly novel. It's not like Carolyn or me or anyone else in the crowd thought this sound was something special. Hadn't we already been through enough, what with the unexpected ringing of the church's bell and the distressing burning of the mill's office?

All the same, we listened as the sound moved off the river's bank. The sound then headed toward the middle of the river, and then it turned downriver toward the dam.

Soon a battered aluminum fishing boat came into view. The boat had been obscured by the mill, but now it was out in the open. It looked to be a fourteen-footer, and its old Tecumseh outboard was just chugging away.

The boat was riding low in the water. Someone had carefully piled wooden crates in the boat, because without such care, this boat most certainly would have listed to one side and begun to take on water. Without such care, this boat would have gone to the bottom of the river.

But instead of sinking, this battered aluminum fishing boat with its ballast of wooden boxes was now chugging along low in the water. This sight caused us to move upriver above the dam. We didn't really think about why we began to move; it was just something we did together.

As we walked, we expected the boat to turn and come toward shore or even come about and head upriver. But that didn't happen, and in a very short time, more and more people realized the little boat wasn't going to turn.

A picture began to form in our heads, one of a future where the current made the engine powerless. Then, the little boat would pick up speed, and when it reached the crest of the dam, the back of the boat with its engine would flip skyward, and the little boat and crates and driver would disappear into the plunge pool of the dam.

We all held our breath and watched our picture come to pass. The little boat reached the crest. The little boat flipped. Carolyn screamed, "Oh, shit, CHARLES!" The little boat disappeared. Then . . .

BANG

THE DAM

BLEW UP

After the Blast

Just after the dam blew up, the river pushed through the hole created by the blast. The river's water flowed downstream and flooded up over In Street. The water continued up against the hill and then down over the creek's mouth and up the creek's channel.

We who answered the ringing of the church's bell, who attended the burning of the mill, and who witnessed the bombing of the dam stood safely upriver. And like us, Wildcat too lay unharmed. The town across the river was spared because it was on higher ground. Even Hotel Wildcat went unscathed. Being directly across from the dam, it marked the flood's high-water mark.

The blast turned the center of the dam into rubble. Pieces of concrete were forced by the pressure of the flood over to the river's new boundaries. There were bigger pieces close by and smaller bits downriver, and one large chunk came to rest just down and across from Hotel Wildcat.

Not Much to Say

In no time the river behind the dam emptied downstream. We who had come down to the river, many from Wildcat and a few from the hill, began to murmur among ourselves.

Some turned and walked back into Wildcat. I saw my parents make their way to Out Street and head up the hill. Others just stayed. I guess the shock was too much.

And then there was Dominic. He had been with Carolyn and me just as the last of the fire was put out. After that we lost track of him, what with Charles ending his life by blowing a hole in the dam. Somewhere in that confusion, Dominic must have gone somewhere. I looked about, but I couldn't find him.

Carolyn's hand felt very small in mine. Her fingers were balled together. They felt like a baby animal, maybe a baby bird in an egg, my hand the shell, hers the embryo.

After shouting, "Oh, shit, Charles," Carolyn didn't say anything else. I thought I knew what her shout meant, and I thought everyone else did, too. There wasn't anything else to say.

I started to walk Carolyn home, although she didn't say she wanted to go home. With the remnants of the dam at our backs, we walked between Hotel Wildcat and the mill and up Out Street. We passed School Street and then Church Street until we came to White Damp Way, where we turned left.

We stopped just outside Carolyn's house. We stood quietly for a moment holding hands. We didn't know what to say, so we just stood without saying anything and waited for the future to swallow us whole. We didn't know what else to do.

Carolyn's house was only four feet off the road, but I thought it seemed flatter and emptier than I had remembered. Peelings of battleship-gray paint lay at the foot of the basement door.

I had been inside Carolyn's house many times, and yet I had trouble believing anyone lived there. It felt like one of those empty houses you pass that has given up being a house. Once the house had been a place for families. Meals were cooked in its kitchen. Conversations were spoken in its living room. Dreams were had night after night in its bedrooms. But then the house was neglected, starved, and the house didn't have the energy to keep a family warm and safe anymore. A husk of a house.

"I'll come inside with you," I finally said.

"No."

"But you'll need to . . ."

"No."

"Ah, what about Charles? I'd like to . . ."

"No," and Carolyn turned, opened the basement door, and disappeared inside.

I felt like something had changed. I didn't know exactly what it was, but that's how I felt. Oh, I knew about the fire at the mill and the explosions at the mine and the dam, and I knew that three miners had died. I knew those were huge changes. And I knew Charles was dead, but it was something else.

I wasn't sure, but all the same, I felt fairly certain.

WHAT WAS SAID

A few days later a story began to emerge. It wasn't much, and what was said was simple.

When the mill was closed for good, Charles Zalewski lost his job. He drank for a while, and then he broke into the mine's dynamite magazine, an old stone building with a cast-iron door on rusty hinges. He took a crowbar to the lock, and inside, he found wooden crates of dynamite and cardboard boxes of blasting caps, which he loaded into his hulk of a Chevy Caprice Estate wagon.

On the way to the river, Charles used the same crowbar on the mill's office door, went inside, and set fire to the filing cabinets and furniture. Some said he wanted a crowd.

Although the crowbar was just a theory and there was no direct evidence that he had started the fire, there was little doubt that Charles went to the river, moved the explosives to a battered aluminum fishing boat, rigged up a detonator, and started up the Tecumseh motor. And there was even less doubt that once Charles was out in the river, he headed for the dam.

LAST TIME

The next time I saw Carolyn she was down at the river's edge, just below the remains of the dam. It was a cloudy, humid day, the sort where the Gulf of Mexico comes up and exhales its damp breath right in your face.

Carolyn was sitting on the large chunk of concrete that had just recently come to rest down from Hotel Wildcat. She was wearing cutoff jeans and a white cotton peasant blouse. She was twirling a strand of her long hair and seemed to be looking into the hole that her brother's blast had left in the dam.

"Mind if I hop up next to you?" I was trying to be cheery.

"Okay."

"I've missed you." I tried sincere.

"Uh-huh."

"Thinking about Charles?"

"Uh-huh."

Because it seemed like the right thing to do, I asked about Charles, and Carolyn told me that when she was little, Charles would take her on walks around Wildcat and later up and across the hill. He taught her about the good mushrooms like chanterelles, oysters, and chicken of the woods and the bad mushrooms like fool's funnels, yellow stainers, and death angels. He gave her a small penknife for harvesting, and they would hunt together.

And because her father was an angry drunk, Carolyn said that, as she grew, she relied more and more on Charles. Their walks grew longer in both time and distance. Charles taught Carolyn how to find and harvest ramps. She also learned to dig sassafras and make tea. When she was with Charles, childhood was magical.

Unfortunately, Carolyn's father was killed in a hunting accident. At least that was the story. Her father was unreliable and not well-liked, but he had once been a Wildcat boy, and then he was a Wildcat man who worked at the mill. That had to count for something. At least until it didn't.

After that, everything changed. Charles stopped going to school. He got a job at the mill. Maybe it was his father's job and maybe it wasn't, but now Charles was the one who got up in the morning, went to the mill, picked up his paycheck, brought it home, and then popped open a bottle of beer.

As it turned out, Carolyn didn't just lose her father, she also lost her brother. No more hunting for mushrooms. No more foraging for ramps. No more digging sassafras. No more feeling that someone gave a damn.

"I don't know what to say," I said.

"Uh-huh."

"You and your mom aren't having a memorial service for Charles?" I asked.

"For what? For my asswipe brother who blew a hole in the dam?"

"Sorry, I guess not. I guess this is Charles's memorial service."

"I guess so."

Then, we were quiet for a bit. Carolyn continued to twirl her hair and look into the hole in the dam. I wanted to somehow make things better, but I couldn't, so I watched an ant struggle with something larger than itself. It was having a hard time, too.

"Not to change the subject, but my dad says he's got a new job. He says he knew the mill was closing for a while, and it was his job to get all the paperwork in order, but since all that got burned, there isn't any reason for him to stay."

"Uh-huh."

"I guess what I'm trying to say is that they'll be moving soon."

"Uh-huh." And Carolyn stopped twirling her hair. She turned to face me. Her eyes narrowed. "So?"

"Uh, I'm not sure . . ."

"And you?"

"Oh, I'm going with them. I'll go to college where my dad's new job is."

And with that Carolyn slid off the chunk of concrete and walked toward Hotel Wildcat and then up Out Street. I slid off the chunk of concrete, too, but I didn't follow her. Instead, I watched Carolyn, the girl I was drawn to and felt for and wanted, walk away. Her body became smaller and smaller, and finally her body turned onto White Damp Way and disappeared.

It was our last time together.

DEAR NEW KID

I was pregnant.
Thought you'd like to know.
Now I'm not.

CAROLYN

Into the Future

Back in Hotel Wildcat, I've just finished writing about the dam and the terrible things that happened a very long time ago, and now, I feel more in tune with Wildcat's past. Oh, not in the way that Wildcat's lifelong residents do, that's a place reserved just for them, but more in tune all the same.

I lay down my turkey quill, wait a moment for Arabelle's mushroom ink to dry on Rocco's mushroom paper, and then bring all the pages together into a single stack to make sure they are in order. I like the way they all live together, and I set them aside on my sassafras table.

But the good feeling doesn't last because I know Dominic will ask again about my unfinished business. Yes, I'm quite sure he will ask if I've seen Carolyn.

I go to the window and look down to the dam and the hole that Charles made. After the explosion, it was decided not to repair the dam. Some people said that the time for river barges was over, and because the dam served no other purpose, really, what was the point?

I watch the water come lazily down. A few summer rocks have appeared, and I wonder if the water level will drop even farther. Soon, I'll be able to walk to the other side, the way people once did before someone built the dam.

I go back to my table and think about Carolyn and all that I have written about the young woman I knew a long time ago. I also wonder about the Carolyn that Dominic said I should talk to. Where has she traveled and who has she met? Has she married, and are there children? I haven't heard that Carolyn is with someone. Is she alone in her mother's house, the place where she grew up, where her brother once said to me, "Kill us one way or another."

I lay out a fresh piece of paper, pick up my quill, dip it in some ink, and then lay my quill back down. Instead of writing, I think I'll go for a walk. Of course, I'll return periodically and write about it, all the while relying on that element of trust you and I have built up.

Think of this as the introduction to an account of my walk into the future. Maybe I'll bump into Carolyn; wouldn't that be something. Maybe I won't, and there I'll find Dominic, asking me why not.

PASTA

I left my room and smelled good things cooking in the kitchen. I thought it might be something Italian: garlic and oregano and basil mixed with the brightness of tomatoes.

I walked down the stairs, went into Hotel Wildcat's tavern, and sat down. The place was empty, but soon it would be time for dinner, and everyone who lived in Hotel Wildcat would come in the tavern door or through the side door that leads from the lobby. I looked forward to seeing them.

Often Friday is pasta night at Hotel Wildcat. It all starts with Donald and Alexander going across the river and visiting the Italian grocery. There they choose from bucatini, *capelli d'angelo*, farfalle, fusilli, gnocchi, lasagna, *mezzi*, pappardelle, *rotelle*, spaghetti, vermicelli, *zita*; you get the picture. Both linguine and fettuccine are customary, although I remember a couple of different nights when we had penne, and once there was rigatoni.

I had no idea what Donald and Alexander would choose, but for some reason I thought it might be *conchiglietti rigate*, which is large shells. I don't know why I thought we were having shells, as we'd never had shells before, but that's what I thought.

"Hey stranger," Arabelle said, entering the tavern and walking to our table. "Where've you been all day? I didn't see you at lunch." She was wearing a blue-on-rust paisley blouse with jeans. She'd pulled her hair back behind a cheetah-print bandanna.

"Writing," I answered.

"You've been doing a lot of that lately." She sat down next to me. "Careful you don't get lost."

"That's fair. All out of breadcrumbs, so I left sassafras shavings."

"That's good. Need any more ink?"

"Now that you mention it, I could use a refill. I guess I'll need to see Rocco, too."

"Sounds like a plan."

After I sorted out my writing needs with Arabelle, Leonard came in and sat down across from me. Soon, all the other residents came in, too, and there was quite a buzz with this one talking to that one. Everyone quieted down when Donald came out of the kitchen, followed by Alexander. Each had a platter of pasta.

After serving two of the tables, Donald and Alexander went back to the kitchen and brought out two more platters. Donald took his platter to the table at the back of the tavern, and Alexander brought his platter to our table, the one in front of the window, the place with the best view of the river.

As it turned out, I was right. Donald and Alexander had piled large shell-shaped pasta on the platter. The shells were stuffed with a mixture of cheeses from the dairy, and marinara sauce was poured over the top. The sauce was made from plum tomatoes, ones that were freshly picked from Anthony's garden.

Anthony keeps an extensive garden upriver beyond Floreandra's hives. It's the place where the gypsies set up camp during the terrible time when the mill closed for good, and now it's where Anthony grows the tomatoes, radicchio, leeks, garlic, sweet peppers, and carrots that his Italian ancestors passed down to him as well as the red cabbage, rutabagas, turnips, and beets that his eastern European neighbors have asked for.

A few days ago, while Anthony was tending his garden, I heard Rocco yell, "Hey, truck farmer, when're you going to get a truck?"

Anthony yelled back, "I don't got no truck with the likes of you, *produttore di carta.*"

Then, they both laughed.

I didn't get the joke, so that evening I asked Anthony what was all that about trucks, and he said, "You know there was truck farming before there was trucks."

"But I still don't get it, Anthony."

"It's not truck; it's *troque.* It's French, means to barter."

"Oh, like farmers trading vegetables, but how do you know all this?"

"Way back, my momma's family were farmers down in Louisiana."

"But you're Italian, not French."

"So?" and I had to admit he had me there.

Dinner started when Leonard took a serving spoon and scooped three shells onto his plate. Those of us who live at Hotel Wildcat always wait for Leonard to help himself. It is something that we do for Leonard, an honor that is all his own, and now that Leonard had served himself, the rest of us did, too.

We all must have been hungry because, after some more buzz, the room was quiet again except for words like "please pass the" and "thank you." The shells were a perfect al dente, the cheeses creamy, and the marinara had that characteristic Donald and Alexander balance of sweet and acid and spice.

Right about the time most of us were starting in on our second shell, Dominic came in and sat down.

"Thought you might miss out," Arabelle said through a mouth full of cheese.

"Yeah, Dominic, shells," Leonard said, not looking up from his plate.

I stopped eating. Dominic usually isn't late for dinner. I knew something was up and that soon Dominic would clue us in, but I wasn't sure how long it might take.

While I waited, everyone in the room also stopped eating, except for Leonard, that is. He decided to use the silence as an opportunity to spoon a fourth shell onto his plate.

"Okay, spill it," I said. "We wouldn't want Donald and Alexander to think it's their food." I didn't want to sound patronizing, but I did all the same. I guess I couldn't help it.

Dominic looked toward the river and answered, "You really should talk to her."

On Edge

After Dominic told me to see Carolyn, I nodded, and then dinner continued. Everyone went back to eating, but the meal felt rushed. Everyone knew what Dominic wanted me to do, and until I did what he asked, interactions in Hotel Wildcat would be on edge, especially for me.

We knew mealtime was over when Leonard stabbed his last piece of shell, dragged it through the remaining marinara sauce, and lifted the dripping shell to his mouth.

After he swallowed, Leonard said, "Shells," got up from his chair, pushed it under the table, and left the tavern.

Another of The Shadows

I was now the center of attention, something I've never liked. I prefer either to be in conversation with one or two good friends or off by myself walking or writing. I really enjoy lunch and dinner because I always look forward to seeing Dominic, Arabelle, and Leonard. When it comes to socializing, that's about my limit.

But now my good friend Dominic had publicly called me out, and as is my inclination when I'm agitated, I walked back to my room. I went to the window and watched the river. I followed a large tree branch as it floated by, and then there were a few ducks working an eddy, and suddenly something surprising caught my eye, one of The Shadows, one I hadn't seen before. Needless to say, I was filled with questions. Was The Shadow new? And if so, a person must have died, someone who I might have known, but now this person was dead, nothing left to do but mourn. Or maybe The Shadow was not new at all. Maybe it had been there for a very long time, and for some reason, I hadn't noticed until now.

I was curious because The Shadow was atop the large chunk of concrete which had been blown free from the dam, washed up on the beach, and now sat just down from Hotel Wildcat. The Shadow wasn't looming over the chunk of concrete, and it didn't obscure it in any way. It was as if The Shadow had come ashore on a boat, and after disembarking, had taken a fancy to the chunk of concrete and decided to sit down and rest for a while.

I felt there was something meditative about The Shadow. Maybe it was The Shadow of a Buddhist monk who wandered this way and then another way across the hill. Later, The Shadow went on to gather ramps in a moist, secret spot. Then at some point, The Shadow continued down to the creek to where the dark movements of otters came together and parted and came together again. But now The Shadow was here, and I was looking at it from my Hotel Wildcat window.

SOMETHING I HAD TO DO

After wondering about The Shadow, I became restless. I didn't want to stay in my room, so I left Hotel Wildcat, walked from In Street over to Out Street, and followed Out Street toward the hill.

I really didn't know where I was going. As I walked, the sun stretched my shadow up the road, and the licorice scent of hyssop drifted down to me on the breeze. I listened to the cicadas go at it like scissors on a grindstone.

When I got beyond White Damp Way and came to the big bend in Out Street, I turned around to take in the full panorama. The homes of Wildcat were to my right, and the mill and Hotel Wildcat were directly below. To my left, the cows were returning to the dairy, and when I looked beyond, I could imagine the creek.

Then, Carolyn entered the picture. She appeared where White Damp Way meets Out Street, and from there, she turned and headed away from me toward the river. I wasn't surprised to see her. I knew that seeing her was something I had to do, no way to avoid it, and now it was about to happen.

Be that as it may, I didn't know whether Carolyn wanted to see me. I knew there was an element of danger. What if she had no interest? Or maybe she would stand and scold me, or even worse, she might refuse to acknowledge that I was here at all. What would I do then?

Finally, I decided to put those worries in my pocket and start walking back into town, and when I reached Hotel Wildcat, I could see that Carolyn had stopped at the river. She was standing next to the large chunk of concrete, the one that her brother Charles had blown free from the dam. Then, she pushed herself up on the chunk, and soon she was sitting and looking at the river, the one that came down to and flowed away from Wildcat.

From where I was standing, I could see The Shadow, the one that I'd seen from my Hotel Wildcat window. I could also see that Carolyn was sitting next to The Shadow. She was a couple of inches shorter, and there was just enough room for the two of them.

THE SHADOW OF HER SMILE

I decided to take my chances, head down to the river, and talk with Carolyn. I didn't know what the future would bring. I didn't know whether she would smile, or when she saw that I was back, would she decide that she didn't care about any of that? I just didn't know.

As I came down to the river, I began to feel that The Shadow, the one on the chunk of concrete next to Carolyn, was Charles. I wondered why I hadn't felt this before. Had The Shadow come right after Charles blew the hole in the dam? If so, then I hadn't seen it. Or had The Shadow somehow been summoned when Carolyn came home? Or maybe it was Carolyn who let me see The Shadow. I thought it was all quite mysterious.

When I got close enough, Carolyn said, "Hop up, new kid."

Hearing her voice after all these years was unsettling, but all the same, I did as I was told. I pushed myself up so that my back was to Carolyn's shoulder, and I was looking down the river toward the creek. There wasn't room for me to face the river.

"Long time," I said.

"Uh-huh."

"Dominic told me, no actually ordered me, to talk to you."

"Uh-huh."

"You're not going to make this easy, are you?" I asked.

"Uh-uh." And out of the corner of my eye, I thought I saw the shadow of her smile.

CAROLYN'S PAST

I asked Carolyn about the last fifty years or so. I told her that I thought she would always stay in Wildcat, and that, yes, I'd been wrong, and then I asked what prompted her to leave her house and her mother and the river and all that was Wildcat.

She explained that, not long after I left, she got a copy of *Be Here Now*, a book by Ram Dass, and she started taking it down to the creek to read. She said she read it once, and then again, and when she got into it a third time, she figured if I left town, she could, too, which led to her sewing a home-made duffel bag out of an old blanket, packing up her stuff, and hopping on a bus heading west.

She got as far as Bloomington, Indiana, where she stopped, got a job stocking mostly produce in a grocery store, and lived on the cheap by crashing in university students' apartments.

Once she saved enough money for another bus ticket, Carolyn said she grabbed her duffel and continued down the road all the way to Lawrence, Kansas. This time she got a job in a book and antique store called Half as Much, and the manager let her hang some of her art on the wall. Her paycheck wasn't enough for her to find her own place, but a guy who liked her artwork said she could move in with him if he could have one of her drawings. She said he lived above a defunct auto dealership, where he'd set up a one-stop auto mechanics and body shop. She also said she stayed a while because the light was good.

By day, the guy fixed other people's cars, and Carolyn went to work. By night, he fixed his own cars, and she would draw and paint. She even started doing a little bit of sculpture, warty depictions of household objects modeled out of wet newspapers and school glue and colored with various auto shop grimes and Bondo dust.

She said this was okay for a bit, but then she hopped on another bus, which took her one state over to Boulder,

Colorado, a place that she said changed her life. She told me that, when she got off the bus, she walked into an old bus depot, and there was Ram Dass speaking to a large group of people. Imagine! Ram Dass and all sorts of other feral types like Allen Ginsberg and Anne Waldman.

That night she hooked up with a bunch of hippies who said they were all part of a new college called Naropa Institute. They said it was to be a Buddhist college right there at the base of the Rocky Mountains, the wall that marks the end of America and the beginning of Benevolent Attentiveness.

After that, she went with the hippies to hear a musician named John Cage. He told the audience that he wanted to quiet their minds so that they might experience divine influence. And he was right; the music that John Cage played was unlike anything Carolyn had ever felt.

Caught up in the Boulder vibe, she went out and got a job waiting tables in a Cantonese restaurant, bounced around Boulder learning to combine meditation and drawing, and hung out with a group of street performers for whom she designed costumes and sculpted props.

She said she stayed in Boulder for almost fifteen years, and then she met a guy who said he was from California and wondered if Carolyn might join his agitprop theater troupe, come to Santa Rosa, and do all things scenery, props, and costumes. Since she was thinking about buying a bus ticket anyway, and since he was paying the way and providing a place to sleep and something to eat, why sure, she was more than happy to get on his little party bus, the one he called Pilot Light.

And all that opened up a new world, one where later Carolyn was asked to go to Moab, Utah, and Spearfish, South Dakota, and Makanda, Illinois, and Summertown, Tennessee, and Asheville, North Carolina, and more recently she worked at the Open'er Festival in Gdynia, Poland, and the Sziget Festival in Budapest, Hungary, and the Exit Festival in Novi Sad, Serbia, and finally, just before she came back to Wildcat, there was some work at the Fringe in Edinburgh, Scotland.

Naturally, when she finished her story, I was at a loss. I mean, the only things I could think of were cliché, and I certainly didn't want to go there, so here we were, quietly sitting on the concrete chunk Charles had blown free from the dam.

After a while, the sun turned the river golden, and its ripples flashed like sparks, and that's when Carolyn asked, "So, what about you, new kid?"

SO, WHAT ABOUT ME?

"Well, would it surprise you that I have never been to Novi Sad? How is Serbia? Can't imagine," I said. "Sounds pretty cool."

"Every place is cool if you live cheap," Carolyn said, and we sat quietly for a little longer. Then, Carolyn asked, "But you're not off the hook. Like I said, what about you?"

"Oh, no globe-trotting, that's for sure. I got an English degree and a teaching certificate and started teaching high school English. My first job was in a Catholic school in upstate New York. The principal died, and they held the wake in the school library. It was one of those open classroom schools, which meant that three of the library's walls were glass. They wheeled him right in at the end of the school day and set him up, open casket and all. The whole school had to walk by the principal's corpse just to get out of the building. Wild, huh?"

"Uh-huh. What else?"

"I only spent a couple years there, and then I left for another school in West Virginia. It was a public school this time, more money, and I got married, but she left me, and I got married again, and I left her."

"Any kids?"

"No, you?" I thought meeting Carolyn's kids might be nice.

"Uh-huh, a son."

"What's his name?"

"Echo."

"Echo, I like that. Where's he now?"

"He's a blacksmith and lives in a commune in the Ozarks. I wanted to have a baby, so I had Echo. He and I went a lot of places, and then, we went different places," Carolyn said and stopped for a moment. A muskrat swimming against the river's current caught her attention, and then she continued, "Hey, not so fast. What about your writing?"

"I've always done some, but I really concentrated on being a good teacher. After a while, I left the school in West

Virginia for a school in northern Pennsylvania. I stayed there a long time. Kind of settled in."

"But then?"

"After my parents died, I got tired of wrangling kids, but maybe I shouldn't blame it on them, because, really, I think I'm just getting old. That's when Dominic told me Hotel Wildcat had reopened, so I retired, and my nest egg and me, well, here we are."

"I see that."

"Dominic told me your mother died," I said. I didn't want the spotlight on me. No, I wanted it on Carolyn.

"Uh-huh."

"And now you're here."

"You can see that. I also see that you're still dumb some-times," and there it was again, her smile.

"I guess you're right."

"Uh-huh."

THE WILDCAT MOON VERSUS THE STARLESS NIGHT

Carolyn and I had traveled the length of our past, and then we were quiet again. She looked out across the river, and I looked down toward the creek. The sunset over the river had left some time ago. For some reason the night was starless, although I didn't remember there being clouds when I left my room. I was a little disappointed that I couldn't see any stars, but I could see the moon. I liked the way the crescent of the moon was a miniature of Carolyn's ear.

The Shadow of Charles was still with us. It was next to Carolyn, and I was beginning to think it came right after Charles came down the river in a fourteen-foot aluminum fishing boat filled with dynamite and blasting caps and blew a hole in the dam. Whether that was true or not, I was pretty sure that The Shadow of Charles was going to be with us from now on.

And just as I was about to ask Carolyn what was next, she hopped off the chunk of concrete, turned to me, and said, "I'm going home now. Come by in the morning sometime. I've got something to show you." Then, Carolyn walked away from the river and up onto Out Street and into the starless night.

SOMETHING

After Carolyn left, I decided to walk down along the river. As I went, I wondered what Carolyn wanted to show me. Maybe it was something she had brought back from her travels or something her mother had left her, possibly something of Charles's, or maybe it was something I had given her a long time ago. Maybe it was something I had written.

Soon enough, I stopped at the place where the creek comes down to the river and sat on the shale bench, the one covered with haircap moss, the one that I like so much.

I thought about Carolyn's long cinnamon hair and the way she had once parted it down the middle. Now, her hair was much shorter, a shaggy bob with bangs. I also remembered the way her large wire-rimmed glasses magnified her sky-blue eyes. Now, her frames were wooden and studded with jewels.

Sitting there, I felt sleep come up from the creek and wrap its arms about me. I knew I should go back to Hotel Wildcat, up to my room, and maybe lie down on my chaise longue. The night was warm, and I wouldn't need a blanket, but I didn't do that. Instead, I lay down on the shale bench and closed my eyes. The haircap moss felt luxuriant, and I fell asleep.

I dreamed I was a beehive at night. Like me, most of the bees were asleep. Only a few young bees gently buzzed. They were caring for the memories stored in each wax cell. They were bhikkunīs of bees.

GALLERY

The sun was already shining in my head before I woke up. My eyes were closed, but my head was filled with bright light, and I was walking through a gallery of sculptures. The gallery had no floor and ceiling, and the walls were nowhere to be seen. The sculptures were not hanging or suspended in any way.

Some of the sculptures were clearly *of* something. One looked like a water glass, but it was made from plaster or papier-mâché, or maybe it was made from something else. I couldn't really tell. Another was a frying pan with two strips of bacon and an egg sunny-side up, and yet another appeared to be a still life arrangement of a dildo dispensing oil into a coffee cup from an antique motor oil can. And there were others that I didn't recognize at all, the sort of art some call abstracts.

I'm not sure why, but I thought that Carolyn had made these sculptures. My mind had created this gallery for me to walk through, and although I hadn't seen Carolyn's artwork for a long time, and she had only told me a little bit about all that was new, here I was walking and enjoying Carolyn's art, some pieces that I thought she had made.

SOUNDS

I heard with my ears before I opened my eyes.

There was a nest of herons across the creek, and the young ones were whooping it up for breakfast.

A gang of crows were going at it. It all started with one crow, and then another one answered, and soon I heard a third from farther away, and suddenly there were so many that I couldn't tell how many there were and from what direction their caws came.

A bug whirred about, and then, *buzzzzzzz*, it came close to my ear. I didn't know what kind of bug it was.

Something dropped, *plop*, nearby.

There was a soft gurgle from the creek, and the wind whispered something among the trees.

When I opened my eyes, I watched a cottonwood leaf drift lazily down.

BREAKFAST

After I opened my eyes, I got up and started my way back to Hotel Wildcat. I went to my room and grabbed a towel and a bar of soap. I thought a good shower before breakfast would feel good. It did.

Breakfast at Hotel Wildcat is a casual thing. Whereas lunch and dinner have set times, breakfast is come as you please. You never know who you might see, something to spice up the morning.

Before any of us get up, Donald and Alexander lay out a simple buffet. There is always a pot of strong coffee and a basket full of loose tea. The baskets are made in the mill by Chéri. She cuts long thin strips from fresh sassafras and weaves them into interesting shapes. The baskets have a delightful fragrance, and we use them to store all that we cherish.

Also, there is a surprise special. Every day the special changes, and today Donald and Alexander had baked raspberry scones. The raspberries had come from Anthony's garden, and there was butter from the dairy mixed with honey from Floreandra's hives.

When I walked into breakfast, I saw Dominic sitting and looking out the window to the river. In front of him was a small plate with a few crumbs and a cup of coffee. Dominic always takes his coffee black, whereas I always add a teaspoon of Floreandra's honey and a splash of the dairy's milk.

I didn't often see Dominic at breakfast. He is an early riser and usually leaves to tend to his mushrooms before I come in, but today I was up earlier than usual, so I had a chance to take my scone and coffee and sit with Dominic.

"Hey, Dominic."

"Hey."

"The river looks nice this morning."

"Yeah, I suppose it does," Dominic said, but he didn't look my way. Instead, he continued to look toward the river. "What are you doing up so early?"

"Carolyn."

"What about Carolyn?" he asked, but I think he already knew.

"I saw her last night."

"Do tell."

"She said she wanted to see me this morning. Said there was something she wanted to show me."

"Go on."

"Do you know anything about this?" I asked.

"Not really," Dominic said and closed his eyes. I wondered what he was seeing, his own version of the river or something else? Then, Dominic opened his eyes, his gaze still out over the river, and he said, "You know much about Carolyn's abortion?"

"Uh, she sent me a letter when I was in college. She said she had an abortion and thought I should know. That's about it."

Dominic turned, made eye contact with me, had a sip of coffee, and turned back to the river. "So, you don't know who went with her. And you don't know who paid?"

"No, I don't."

"Do you want to know?" Dominic asked.

"Of course, it's just that Carolyn never said."

"No, I suppose not. Of course, you didn't ask, but I suppose not. Well, when Carolyn thought she might be pregnant, she came to me. She didn't have any money, and she didn't know what to do. There wasn't any point in asking her mom. Sure, she told her mom, but what was her mom going to do. Her mom didn't really get up off that chair." Then, Dominic stopped, looked to me again, took a sip of coffee, and looked back to the river.

"And what happened?"

"What happened was Carolyn and I talked with my parents, and she said she was scared. She didn't even want to think about it. She said she just wanted it all to go away.

"We told her that we had some money left over from when Luigi got blown up in the mine. She argued a bit, said she didn't want our money, but we insisted, and then, she quit arguing. She said that it sounded all right. I drove

Carolyn in Charles's old wagon to get her checked, and it turned out she was pregnant. Then, I drove her to get an abortion and drove her home."

"I don't know what to say."

"Didn't think you would," Dominic said.

I couldn't take my eyes off Dominic. He couldn't take his eyes off the river. "Thanks, I was pretty useless."

"Was?" Dominic drummed the table with his left hand. The river flowed through the hole Charles had made many years before. "But anyway, I'm glad you're back, and now, you got a date with Carolyn."

"I guess I do."

ON THE WAY

As it turned out, I didn't eat my scone or drink my coffee. Instead, I got up from the table because I had better things to do.

Walking to Carolyn's house brought back many memories. I had just written the memories down and then put them in a drawer. I didn't think this was the time to revisit them, at least not yet. I knew that soon I'd come to Carolyn's house, and I would knock, and she would come, and then things would change, but I had no idea how.

After I turned onto White Damp Way, I came to Carolyn's house. I stopped and stood for a while to take it all in. Someone had painted the basement door with DayGlo colors in a tie-dye pattern and the first story was still red, but someone had hung a striking floral display in a macrame holder. The arrangement had a bird-of-paradise rising majestically through purple verbena while some silver falls cascaded down. It was a living sculpture, and I knew I'd remember it for a long time.

But the biggest change was the disposition of the two small, double-hung windows that peered out toward the river. For the first time, I felt like the house had fully opened its eyes. No, the windows had not been replaced nor had anyone painted the sashes, but the house no longer seemed timid. It was like the house once had a chronic illness, maybe it was lactose intolerant or allergic to peanuts, but now there had been a lifestyle change. Or maybe many, many painful memories had been lifted from the house. Maybe it was something like that.

Just as I went to knock on the basement door, I heard Carolyn's voice call down, "Hey, new kid, door's open."

I turned the knob and went in.

DATE

Carolyn's basement was not how I remembered. Although it was dark and musty and still had boxes piled one upon another, her basement didn't feel like the dust and shadows were whispering my name. For the first time, it felt only like Carolyn's basement.

The stairs up to the kitchen remained rickety, and when I went into the kitchen, I found Carolyn painting the cabinets. She had chosen a light lavender color, and the single window had been washed. The only light in the room was daylight, and there was no cigarette smoke. No dishes or glasses were piled in the sink, and the cast-iron skillet hung on a nail pounded in the wall. It wore the sheen of a clean, well-seasoned pan.

"Hi again," I said.

"Sit down," she said, "I want to finish this cabinet."

Smiling, I sat down and watched Carolyn. She was wearing a pair of black jeans and a faded green T-shirt with the long sleeves rolled up to her elbows.

"Place looks nice," I said. I tried to be cheerful.

"You mean the place was a dump."

"I didn't say that, but I see you're making this place your own."

"Well, this place was a dump, the dumpiest house on the dumpiest street in dumpy Wildcat."

"And now you're back, and now it's not."

"Uh-huh."

I could see that Carolyn had changed. Oh, she was still Carolyn, but once she had been sedimentary rock, most certainly shale, and now she was metamorphic, possibly slate, but the more I considered it, the more I felt she was a sparkly quartzite. At least that's what I preferred.

"Okay, new kid, that should do. I'll just cap the paint, put the brush in a plastic bag, and put the brush in the freezer. After that, I got something to show you."

"Sounds good," and with that Carolyn went about putting her kitchen in order. She didn't make eye contact or anything. Then, she disappeared up to the second floor, and when she came back, she had on a brown baseball cap with a logo that I'd never seen before.

I pointed at Carolyn's hat and asked, "What's that?"

"What's what?"

"The symbol on your hat."

"Still dumb, huh."

"Always."

"No argument there. This symbol's the Chinese character for woman. You got a problem with that?"

"Not really."

"Good, then let's go."

THAT WAY

As we left Carolyn's house, I wondered about the way we might go. We could go down to the river and then maybe downstream to the creek, or we could go up the hill toward where I used to live or possibly along the hill until we came to the mine. If we stopped at the mine, we'd visit with Dominic, and Carolyn would share with us both. And if we didn't stop at the mine, Carolyn and I might even go along the hill in a direction I rarely went except in my dreams.

We went that way.

MEMORIES

Carolyn took me to the end of White Damp Way and then onto a trail I remembered from long ago, the one we first walked to find ramps.

The sun was climbing to its zenith, and a breeze flitted over a knoll and down through the trees. Summer was just beginning, ripening and verdant, and it felt like Carolyn and I were quietly walking through a painting done by some American Romantic, possibly someone from the Hudson River school. For just a little while, death was the furthest thing from my mind.

A few times we climbed around a shale outcropping, and other times we descended into a hollow. More than once we strolled along a flat patch, and occasionally we climbed over or went under a downed tree. While we walked, I appreciated the maples, cherries, hickories, oaks, sassafras, and other trees as well as the mayapples, mitreworts, trilliums, blue and white asters, gingers, jack-in-the-pulpits, and bluebells.

Then, the sun's heat came on, and I began to tire. Maybe Carolyn was taking me farther than I expected, or could it be the years had robbed me of my vitality? I thought about these woods, about my love and their indifference. To me it all seemed a paradox, one that hovered over us like a cloud. Really, what was nature before I was born?

And as I walked and pondered, Carolyn stopped at the top of a low ridge, sat down, and asked, "Well?"

"Ah, well what?"

"Well, I guess you need an engraved invitation. Sit down, new kid."

After I sat down, I saw them, *ramps*, but not just any ramps, *the ramps*, the ones that Carolyn had cut long ago and I had bagged. Some of the leaves were beginning to turn yellow, and others had wilted back altogether, so they didn't look exactly like the same ramps, but from where I sat, the moist declivity was much the same as I remembered. Of course, a few trees had grown considerably, and others were no more, but honestly, I wanted to believe that this was what Carolyn wanted me to see.

For a while, I was filled by memories, so much I'd put away, but I didn't lose myself for long, because suddenly Carolyn said, "No, asswipe, not the ramps. Look over there."

So, I did.

WHAT I SAW

I wasn't prepared for what I saw. Oh, I suppose I should have been, but Carolyn has always called me dumb, and now she had just called me asswipe, words I thought were reserved for her long-passed brother, and I must admit she had a point.

At least I had some context because, several days before,

Dominic had told Arabelle, Leonard, and me something remarkable about The Shadows, something about seeing a new one. He said that this new one had on a robe of light and was smaller than the others. Both he and Leonard agreed that they had never seen such a thing.

Now, I was sitting with Carolyn, and The Shadow that I saw glowed in the shade of a sizable maple. Its core was dark, somewhat darker than the maple's shadow, and The Shadow was smaller than the others that I'd seen so many times before.

Apparently, what Dominic had said at dinner was true. Everyone who had seen The Shadows agreed that Dominic knew the most about them. We all knew he was intimately acquainted with The Shadows in ways we did not understand.

And although I couldn't explain what I was seeing, I didn't look away either. There was something childlike, something familiar, and something disquieting, too.

For a good while, I continued to sit and look, and then Carolyn said to me, "Tupela."

It took a few moments for the word to sink in, and then Carolyn took my hand and said again, "Tupela."

"Tupela?" I asked.

"Tupela," Carolyn said, "she's been waiting a long time."

"She?"

"She," and there was a pause that felt like a river of time, one where I was standing on one side of the river and my past was on the other side. Then, Carolyn finished her thought, "Like I said, a long time."

TUPELA

After Carolyn said the thing about Tupela, I got up and crossed the river of time, and as I came close, Tupela did not change in shape or transparency.

When I stopped, I stood very quietly, and as I emptied my mind, I waited for the sound that always comes when I visit The Shadows. I expected to hear a breeze, no, more of a whisper, but not from outside or inside my head, not on the tip of my tongue or even in my ear, and then, ah, there it was, Tupela, but no, sorry for the mistake, this was my own voice, a Tupela of my own making.

And I was really at a loss. So many years, and it had all come to this. Maybe I shouldn't have asked Carolyn what *Topsy-Turvies* was all about, and now here I was again after so long and none the wiser.

Not knowing what else to do, I closed my eyes and softly chanted, "Tupela Tupela, Tupela Zalewski. Tupela Tupela, Tupela Zalewski. Tupela Tupela, Tupela Zalewski," and while I chanted, I began to feel it again, an everlasting patience. I also felt something else, something not precisely a quiver or ripple and not quite electric, but instead a vitality wholly unfamiliar.

Then, I reached out, and in the light, there was warmth, and in the dark, a chill. These feelings were so beyond my experience with The Shadows and yet so similar that I wasn't afraid or anything.

When I stopped chanting, I turned to find Carolyn. I wanted to thank the woman who had brought me here, taken my hand, and said, "Tupela."

I wanted to connect with Carolyn and Tupela, our own little triangle, but apparently that wasn't going to happen because when I looked to where Carolyn had been sitting, she was gone.

THE WAY BACK

The way back to Wildcat was lonely. I don't know what I expected. Maybe I hoped that there'd be a change, that seeing Carolyn would pull the past comfortably into the present. But then again, maybe the river of time only flows one way.

BEES

When I came close to Wildcat, I decided not to walk along White Damp Way. Carolyn had shown me Tupela, and then she had left, so I decided not to pass by her house. Apparently, we were done with seeing each other, at least for the day.

Instead, I walked to the river and continued down until I came to Floreandra's hives. As I passed, I could see her bees leaving and returning. They were busy going about their lives in ways that suited them. I thought there were worse ways to live, and I wondered if the bees would accept me as a disciple. Maybe I could change and become a novitiate, or if not that, at least a postulant. My first step would be to talk to Floreandra. Undoubtedly, she would know how to go about this, and then perhaps I'd find my place. Maybe I'd become a worker in one of her hives. It seemed like an attractive option.

But before I knew it, I had walked past the mill and back to Hotel Wildcat. I could tell something delicious was being prepared in the kitchen, but I didn't recognize the smell. Sometimes Donald and Alexander cook up an unexpected dish for dinner and serve it as a surprise. I thought that this might be one of those times, something to look forward to.

As I headed up the stairs to my room, I heard Leonard exclaim, "Donald, I can't believe it! I mean, is it my birthday, or what?"

SURPRISES

Dinner that night turned out to be quite an affair. I spent the late afternoon putting my walk with Carolyn into words, and when I came down to dinner, everyone but me was seated. They were talking up a storm about what Donald and Alexander had just served, and I had to admit I was surprised, too.

"Didn't see you at lunch, so I saved you a seat," Arabelle said patting the chair next to her, the place where I always sit.

As I settled in, I noticed that Leonard was softly chewing. This was uncharacteristic because Leonard is a quantity over quality man, a real gourmand. I guess Donald and Alexander had truly outdone themselves. It was like Leonard had found his chewing mantra and was becoming one with his food. From now on he'd have a new name, Phra Leonard, Master of the Three Courses.

"Hey, you going to dish up, or what?" Dominic asked. "I'm not planning on waiting for seconds."

"Oh, hi, Dominic. Pierogies, huh? Wow, what's the occasion?"

"It's a surprise," Arabelle said, passing me a serving dish of pierogies in fresh cream and chive sauce.

"They sure are. This is a first, isn't it?" I asked.

"Yes, it is, and, no, this isn't the only surprise," Arabelle said, smiling at no one in particular. I knew something was up because Arabelle wasn't smiling at Dominic or Leonard or me or even Donald and Alexander. Instead, she was smiling at everything and nothing. She was just smiling.

"Do I get a clue?" I asked.

"Nope, just enjoy your meal," Arabelle said.

"Yeah, shut up and eat," Dominic echoed.

Not wishing to argue, I dished up a full plate, and after I cut into the first pierogi and began to chew, I concluded that Donald and Alexander had outdone themselves, each pierogi artfully handmade, each fried in sweet, sweet butter and swirled in velvety sauce. I tried to remember eating anything so delicious. Nothing came to mind.

"Damn, this is good. What's the filling?" I really wanted to know.

"Some of Dominic's oyster mushrooms. He marinated them in oil with rosemary, oregano, and salt," Arabelle said chewing.

"There's some spice, too," I said.

"Oh, I forgot," Arabelle said and wiped her mouth on her napkin, "there's some minced Hungarian wax peppers."

"Damn, Dominic, very nice."

"High praise from you, my friend. High praise," Dominic smiled.

Before long the pierogies and their attendant pickles were gone, and soon dessert would come forth from the kitchen. In the meantime, I watched Donald walk over to Arabelle. He whispered something in her ear, and she nodded in response.

Clearly, something was going on, and just as clearly, I had no idea what it was. I looked over at Dominic, and he winked, a gesture which almost knocked me off my chair. Dominic? Winking? What in the world could possibly come next? World peace? Universal enlightenment? A gentle rain?

And that's when Arabelle gave me a little squeeze on the shoulder and stood up. She was almost giddy when she said,

"Hey, dinner pals, before we have dessert, I just want you to know. Me and Dominic are getting married."

Gasp. Oh, it wasn't a bad sort of gasp. No, it was more like the angels had just found out that, yes, Gabriel, the Second Coming is just around the corner and, yes, Raphael, you get to be a part of it, too. And after the gasp, everyone stood and broke out in applause, everyone except Dominic, who just sat looking very sheepish, something that was another surprise.

PREPARATIONS

Preparations for Arabelle and Dominic's wedding started the next morning. The wedding was to be a Wildcat wedding for Wildcat people in Wildcat style. There would be a ceremony and a reception with lots of dairy, vegetables, ramps, and honey. Floreandra would place beeswax candles all around, and when it came to the invitations, Carolyn agreed to do the calligraphy using Arabelle's mushroom ink on Rocco's mushroom paper. Of course, Dominic would supply all manner of mushrooms.

Arabelle said that she wanted an evening wedding. She wanted their vows to be recited just when the sun set the river ablaze. She had very definite ideas, and at lunch the next day, she said, "Dominic, let's have the wedding in front of the mine."

To be honest, we were all surprised because no one had ever thought of having a wedding in such a place. We wondered what Arabelle was thinking and if Dominic would agree to such a thing. We all knew Dominic wasn't one to go along just to get along even if Arabelle was the one talking and the subject was Arabelle's wedding.

Not surprisingly, we all waited to hear what Dominic had to say, and we could see that this was as much a surprise to him as it was to us, but eventually he put down his salad fork, smiled, and asked, "What else, honey?"

"You know I want Floreandra's candles everywhere, and I think her candles would look nice outside the mine. I'd really like that."

"I can see that," Dominic responded.

"I know we want all of our friends and family to be there, but don't you think it would be nice if some of The Shadows were there, too?"

"I don't know, Arabelle. I hadn't really thought about it."

"No?"

"No, but I guess it's okay."

"We'll have candles all the way down the hill to Hotel Wildcat, and after the ceremony, the sun will have gone down, so we'll walk through candlelight down to the reception. What do you think of that?"

"Sounds good to me."

"Then it's settled, Dominic?"

"Sure, honey, if it's what you want."

WHAT WE WORE

The day of the wedding came, and all of Wildcat got ready in Wildcat style. We understood that this was Arabelle and Dominic's wedding. This wasn't a church wedding. This wasn't great grandma or grandma or ma's wedding. This wasn't out of a magazine, and it certainly wasn't out of an etiquette book. This was to be a Wildcat wedding, and as this was for Arabelle and Dominic, that's the way it would be.

Carolyn's invitations instructed us to wear clothing in colors that suited us. Floreandra dressed in a yellow-and-black-striped T-shirt with matching pajama pants, and because that wasn't enough, she topped it all off with a woven beehive hat.

Chéri stained a white peasant blouse and white jeans the lovely color of sassafras tea, and then, because Dougie and Terence's fashion sense was strictly utilitarian, she did the same for them.

Not surprisingly, Donald and Alexander went all out. Donald's shirt had a collage of broccolis, and his pants were a cheesy yellow. Not to be outdone, Alexander's shirt had a collage of lemons, and his pants were a meringuey white with brown cuffs.

Appropriately, Mary Kay and John donned Jersey brown shirts, Jersey cream pants, and Jersey brown-and-cream-striped jackets, and not to be outdone by Floreandra, they also sported flat-topped Breton caps.

Anthony wore a green suit with a tomato red shirt, and Leonard, well, he wore his threadbare jeans with a white T-shirt, one stained by the leavings of many meals.

Then, there was Rocco. Clearly Rocco wanted to make a statement, so he began by asking Dominic for some mushroom leather, and after cutting the leather into pieces, he sewed them into a tunic and kilt.

When he was done, Rocco asked Carolyn to tattoo his creations with Arabelle's ink. He wanted Carolyn to be guided by her own whimsy, and after the wedding, everyone agreed they had never seen anything like it.

As for me, I wore a white linen shirt with a grandfather collar and black jeans, and as for Carolyn, she helped with all the wedding preparations, but after making her contribution, she didn't attend the wedding at all.

PROCESSION

Before the wedding, Floreandra placed candles in a circle around the mine's entrance and along the path that led from Hotel Wildcat to the mine. She did not light the candles. That would happen when Arabelle and Dominic said their vows, and then all of Wildcat would rejoice.

We all met at Hotel Wildcat and waited for the sun to set the river ablaze, so spectacular, and then it did, and we started up the hill. Everyone was dressed in colors that suited them: green, red, orange, yellow, Jersey cream and brown, white, and black. I liked best the color that Chéri chose, a most natural shade of sassafras tea.

We all followed Arabelle, Dominic, and Rocco, he was the one officiating. Rocco had been through so many of Wildcat's changes. He understood where Wildcat had been and where it was now. He didn't claim to know where Wildcat was going, nobody could know that, but he was a part of Wildcat, and Wildcat was a part of him.

While we walked, all of Wildcat's children went off to play tag among the trees. The older children let the younger ones catch them, and the trees played their part by hiding the younger children. There were cherries and maples, a few oaks and hickories, and as we neared the mine, there was a small stand of sassafras and a single tupelo.

THE WEDDING

When we were all gathered at the entrance to the mine, Floreandra began arranging. She placed Arabelle, Dominic, and Rocco in a triangle, and then she asked everyone else to form a line. Once we were in position, she told one end of the line to connect with the triangle, and when that was achieved, she directed the other end of the line to create a spiral by walking a large circle around the triangle.

When we were finished, we in attendance looked not only upon Rocco in his tattooed mushroom leather tunic and kilt, but also upon Arabelle and Dominic. The bride and groom wore matching mushroom leather robes, ones constructed by Rocco from Dominic's mushroom leather and tattooed by Carolyn using Arabelle's ink. Their robes were a surprise, and we all felt a good deal of wonder.

And then there were The Shadows. From where I stood, I saw The Shadows of Luigi and Valentin along with a few others. I could not see The Shadow of Abernathy because it was behind me, but I felt it all the same.

Finally, it was time for the wedding, and if you ask me, I thought Rocco looked a little nervous. He had never done anything like this before, but that was of no consequence, and we were all pleased when Rocco looked over his horn-rimmed glasses and asked, "You sure you're all in the right place?"

After wondering about Rocco's question, everyone smiled. We always looked forward to what Rocco had to say, the way he tickled us with his thinking.

"Okay, so the river says we should thank Floreandra for organizing all this and what comes next. Oh, and Carolyn, too, for helping out. And for this getup. I feel like the Wizard of Wildcat. I really do.

"And I don't need to remind any of you that a whole lot's come down the river for a long, long time. Why just this afternoon this piece of driftwood washed up right in front of me," Rocco said pointing to Dominic, "and the damnedest thing happened. This young lady, this one right here, picked up this piece of driftwood."

Arabelle must have liked Rocco's story because she beamed her biggest smile, and as for Dominic, he proudly blushed.

"Oh, and I almost forgot, the river says this young lady and this driftwood want a Wildcat blessing. Can I get a 'Hell, yeah!' from everybody?"

And we all responded, "Hell, yeah!"

"Ah, you can do better than that: 'Hell, yeah!!'"

And we ramped it up, "Hell, yeah!!"

"Now, one more time, only this time dig deep: 'Hell, yeah!!!'"

"HELL, YEAH!!!"

"All right, the river's pretty well satisfied. And now the river wants to know, young lady, if you want to keep this piece of driftwood?"

"You know I do," Arabelle responded.

"Then tell this piece of driftwood why. We're all dyin' to know."

"Because I love him. Most of you know Dominic and I have been together since the day I was born. We played together when we were little, and when we got older, we played together some more. We've never stopped playing together. Really, we haven't," and we all laughed. "This wedding, well, it doesn't change anything, except now I got this memory of being here together with Dominic and all of you. And Dominic has the same memory. And it means the world to me and him. I love you, Dominic. I can't help myself and don't want to."

"Okay then, that was something, young lady. It truly was. The river says it's more than tolerable. But now the river wants to know, piece of driftwood, if you will stay with this young lady?"

"Been waiting sixty-seven years."

"I take that as a 'Hell, yeah.' Now go on, tell this young lady why. Nobody's letting you off the hook."

"What Arabelle said. We been together since the beginning, and that's not going to change. I love you, Arabelle, and everything that goes with it."

"Okay, that's not much, but the river says it'll do," and Rocco slipped something off his right wrist and something else off his left. "Now, here's the triangles. Floreandra tells me that one point on the triangle is Arabelle, and one is Dominic, and the last one's Wildcat. You wear this on its mushroom leather choker as a symbol of all the love that's on the hill right now. So, go ahead, put these on each other, and then let's see a big sloppy kiss, and I mean sloppy."

Right then, I looked about and saw a circle of candles, the ones Floreandra had lit around us, and from there I followed a flickering line of light down the hill to where Floreandra was lighting the last.

And as for The Shadows, they lay softly in the dark's cool embrace.

THE RECEPTION

We followed Arabelle, Dominic, and Rocco down the candlelit path to Hotel Wildcat. Everyone was excited for the reception. Donald and Alexander had put out a spread, and Chéri had found a group of musicians who played eastern European folk music—lots of polkas and waltzes—and as it turned out, they were the children of the musicians who helped her sleep as a child.

After climbing the stairs of Hotel Wildcat, I stopped on the porch and listened to the conversation growing inside. The band cut loose with "I'm Gonna Get a Dummy."

Then, I turned from the reception and looked to the river. Up in the night sky, somebody had broken the moon's pearly plate and splashed out the Milky Way, and down on the beach, Carolyn was sitting on the large chunk of concrete. I wondered why I had not seen her at the wedding and if she would come back to Hotel Wildcat for the reception.

The whole situation was unsettling, and although I knew I should attend Arabelle and Dominic's reception, I didn't feel like being with so many people, especially with

Carolyn sitting down there all alone. Instead, I left the porch and walked down the steps away from Hotel Wildcat.

I stopped short of the river, watching Carolyn and thinking about the way she left Wildcat and then came back. She was the one who was born and grew up here, the one who watched her brother die. And she was the one who I had learned so much from, where to find and harvest ramps and where to dig sassafras and how to make tea.

Long ago we held hands and walked along the river to the creek below the hill, and now Carolyn was sitting on the large chunk of concrete next to The Shadow of Charles.

When I'd had enough thinking, I went down and joined Carolyn. I pushed myself up, and we sat for a good long while.

The sounds of Arabelle and Dominic's reception drifted our way: the talking, the music, the peals of laughter, as well as the buzz of cicadas, the chirp of crickets, and the descent of a single nighthawk.

As for me, I no longer was anxious about seeing Carolyn, and as for her, I think she didn't mind seeing me either. And there was nothing left to say.

LOST SURREAL INTERLUDE

WILDCAT ON A NUTSHELL

Maybe it's because a squirrel gave me hell when I walked outside, his nest high atop a creaky old chestnut.

Or maybe I woke up in a sleepover bed, and I didn't know what smelled so good, turned out there were kolacky baking, something to be explored.

Or the leaves were falling orange, yellow, red.

Or an old man kept a big garden while his wife sat in the window. She was paralyzed with dementia, and the old ladies came to fill their baskets.

Or a mudpuppy lay motionless in my hand.

Or the nonni walked to the grocery, and the loaves in the bakery were only fifty cents, their bodies piled all the way to the tin ceiling.

Or the fly ash belched from the mill's stack and rained black from the night sky.

Or I watched an uncle wrap his arms around her, drunk, stepping all over her wedding dress. He could have said he was sorry, shown her just a shadow of shame.

Or a badling of ducks came through Wildcat, and a babcia swept up a drake and slapped his neck across a stump, chop, and drained the blood into some vinegar at the bottom of the soup pot. Her grandson then plucked the body and put the feathers in a paper sack, and the pot, the duck, some water, a few roots, and a handful of dried fruit, all of these, were set to boil.

Or a chipmunk sat on a rock wall and opened an acorn, but then the chipmunk was gone, its mind changed, and now there was a broken acorn splashed with sunlight resting on the rock wall.